KU-744-788

Annie O'Neil spent most of her childhood with her leg draped over the family rocking chair and a book in her hand. Novels, baking, and writing too much teenage angst poetry ate up most of her youth. Now Annie splits her time between corralling her husband into helping her with their cows, baking, reading, barrel racing (not really!) and spending some very happy hours at her computer, writing.

Also by Annie O'Neil

London's Most Eligible Doctor
One Night, Twin Consequences
The Nightshift Before Christmas
Santiago's Convenient Fiancée
Her Hot Highland Doc
Healing the Sheikh's Heart

Italian Royals miniseries

Tempted by the Bridesmaid
Claiming His Pregnant Princess

Discover more at millsandboon.co.uk.

CLAIMING HIS PREGNANT PRINCESS

BY
ANNIE O'NEIL

MILLS & BOON

First published in Great Britain 2017
by Mills & Boon, an imprint of HarperCollins*Publishers*
1 London Bridge Street, London, SE1 9GF

Large Print edition 2018

ISBN: 978-0-263-07254-9

MIX
Paper from
responsible sources
FSC® C007454

This book is produced from independently certified FSC™ paper to ensure responsible forest management. For more information visit www.harpercollins.co.uk/green.

Printed and bound in Great Britain
by CPI Group (UK) Ltd, Croydon, CR0 4YY

This book is dedicated to my great friend Jess. She had the most epic hen do in the history of hen parties and somehow we ended up in a three-mile parade in the centre of a town just outside of Venice. As you do when you're dressed as a nun and the lawfully intended is dressed as a minx. I mean bride.

Big love, Annie O' xx

CHAPTER ONE

"DR. JESOLO! THERE'S a full waiting room!"

"*Si, pronto*, Teo!" Bea poked her head out of the curtained exam space and then repeated herself in English, just in case her Australian co-worker hadn't understood. "On my way."

He nodded, screwed his nose up for a minute and gave her a funny look.

She hoped her pasted-on happy face simply looked like a case of first-day jitters.

Her new colleague didn't need to know she was fighting another wave of impossible-to-quench tears.

She swiped at her eyes again and forced herself to tune in to the various conversations happening in the exam areas surrounding hers.

English, Italian, French and German. Broken arms. Asthma attacks. Altitude sickness. They were all mingled together up here in Torpisi, and she was loving every moment of it. Or would be if she could get her eyes to dry and see another patient.

That was why this multilingual, brain-stretching trauma center suited her needs to a tee.

Hormones or history. It was always a toss-up as to which would unleash the next flood.

You can do this. You're a princess! Trained in the art of...of artifice.

At least work would give her poor over-wrung tear ducts a break.

The Clinica Torpisi catered to the needs of international tourists. Ones who didn't read the gossip rags. Adrenaline junkies, fun seekers and good old-fashioned holidaymakers kept the *clinica* operating on full steam over the summer—and probably more so in the winter, when the skiing crowd came in. It was the perfect place to hide in plain sight. And to create some much-needed distraction from her real-life problems.

Zurich, Lyon, Salzburg and even Milan were only a couple of hours' drive away, but the press still hadn't caught wind of the fact that she was up here in this magical Italian mountain hideaway.

Ha! Foiled again. Just the way she liked it.

They'd had their pound of flesh after the wedding nightmare. Painting a picture of her as if she'd been abandoned at the altar… The cheek! She'd been made of fool of, perhaps, but *she'd* been the one to pull off her ring and walk away.

The press might have stolen what little dignity Bea had left, but she wouldn't let them take away her precious Italy. Especially now that returning to England was out of the question.

Her fingers pressed against her lips as the strong sting of emotion teased the back of her nose again.

Ugh. She'd tried her best to shake off those memories. The ones she'd kept locked away the day since she'd agreed to her mother's harebrained plan. What a fool she'd been!

She'd had a shot of living the perfect life and had ruined it in a vainglorious attempt to please her blue-blooded family. Power and position. It was all they'd wanted.

Well…they'd hit the tabloids, all right, just not in the way anyone had anticipated.

Hopefully the paparazzi were now too busy jetting around the globe trying to find "Italy's favorite playboy prince" to worry about *her* any longer.

Bea pulled the used paper off the exam table and stuffed it in the bin. It was her own fault this mess had blown up in her face. If she'd stayed strong, told her parents she was in love with someone else…

Inhale. Exhale.

That was in the past now. She'd made the wrong decision and now she was paying for it.

Bea took a quick scan of the room, then glanced in the mirror before heading out for her next patient, smiling ruefully as she went. Trust an Italian clinic in the middle of nowhere to have mirrors everywhere! She was willing to bet the hospital on the Austrian side of town didn't have a single one. Practical. Sensible. More her style. Maybe she should have tried to get a job there…

Her eyes flicked up to the heavens, then down again.

Quit second-guessing yourself! It's day one, and so far so good.

She forced herself to look square into the mirror at the "new" Bea.

No more Principessa Beatrice Vittoria di Jesolo, fiancée of Italy's favorite "Scoundrel Prince."

Her eyes narrowed as she recataloged those memories. Everything happened for a reason, and deep in her heart she knew marrying for tradition rather than for love would have been a huge mistake. Even if it would have made her mother happy.

A mirthless laugh leapt from her chest.

She was well and truly written out of the will now!

She shrugged her shoulders up and down, then gave her cheeks a quick pinch.

Saying goodbye to that life had been easy.

The hard part was living with herself after having let things go as far as they had.

"Dr. Jesolo?"

Bea started, and wagged her finger at herself in the mirror.

Self-pity wasn't going to help either. Work would.

"Si, sto arrivando!"

From today she was simply Dr. Bea Jesolo,

trauma doctor to the fun-loving thrill seekers up here in Italy's beautiful Alpine region.

She tipped her head to the side. Now that she was a bit more used to it, she liked the pixie haircut. The gloss of platinum blond. It still caught her by surprise when she passed shop windows, but there were unexpected perks. It made her brown eyes look more like liquid shots of espresso than ever before. Not that she was on the market or anything. Just get up, work, go to bed and repeat. Which made the short, easy-to-style cut practical. Much better than the long tresses she'd grown especially for the wedding.

She gave a wayward strand a tweak, then made a silly face at herself when it bounced back out of place.

Undercover Princess.

That was this morning's newspaper headline. She'd seen it on the newsstand when she'd walked into work. There had been a picture of heaven knew who on the front page of Italy's most popular gossip magazine. A shadowy photo showing someone—no doubt a model wearing a wig—looking furtively over her shoulder as she was swept through airport security in Germany. Or was it Holland? Utrecht? Somewhere *she* wasn't.

Undercover Princess, indeed.

She pulled her stethoscope back into place around her neck and shrugged the headline away.

It was a damn sight better than the handful she'd seen before sneaking away to lick her wounds on her brother's ridiculous superyacht for six weeks, ducking and dodging the press among the Greek islands.

There were perks to having a privileged family. And, of course, pitfalls.

Abandoned by the Wolf!

Prince Picks Fair Maid over Princess!

Altar-cation for Italy's Heartbroken Princess.

Heartbroken? Ha! Hardly.

Love-Rat Prince Crumbles at the First Hurdle

That was getting closer. Or maybe:

Pregnant Principessa Prepares for First Solo as Mama.

Not that anyone knew *that* little bit of tabloid gold.

Doctor by day…

Her hand crept to her belly. Though she wasn't showing yet, she knew the little tiny bud of a baby was in there…just the size of an apple seed. Maybe a little more? Bigger, smaller… Either way she'd protect that blossoming life with every ounce of power she possessed. Hers and hers alone. How she'd go about living the rest of her life once the baby was born was a problem she hadn't yet sorted, but she'd get there. Because she didn't have much of a choice.

Bea swiped at her eyes, forced on a smile, then pulled open the curtain. Nothing like a patient to realign her focus.

"Leah Stokes?"

She scanned the room, bracing herself against the moment that someone recognized her, air straining against her lungs. Her shoulders dropped and she blew a breath slowly past her lips as all the patients looked up, shook their heads, then went back to their magazines and conversations. All except a young twentysomething woman, who was pushing herself up from her chair. She was kitted out in cycling gear and… *Oh. Ouch!*

"Looks like some serious road rash there." Bea's brow furrowed in sympathy and she quickly walked over to the woman and put her arm around her waist. "Lean on me. That's right. Just put your arm around my shoulder and let me take some of the weight."

"I don't think I can make it all the way." Leah drew in a sharp breath, tears beginning to trickle down her cheeks now that help was here.

"Can I get a hand?" Bea called out.

There were a couple of guys in rescue uniforms at the front desk. She called again to get their attention. When the closest one looked up, the blond…

Her breath caught in her throat.

He wasn't blond. His hair was hay colored—that was how she'd always remembered it… The color of British summertime.

A perfect complement to startling green eyes.

As their gazes grazed, then caught, Bea's heart stopped beating. Just…*froze*.

She'd know that face anywhere. It had been two long years. Two painfully long years of trying to convince herself she'd done the right thing, all the while knowing she hadn't.

Fate had intervened in saving her from a loveless marriage, but what was it doing *now*?

Taunting her with what she could never have?

She blinked and looked again.

Those green eyes would haunt her until the end of time.

Before she could stop herself she spoke the name she'd thought she'd never utter again.

"Jamie?"

For a moment Jamie thought he was hallucinating. It *couldn't* be her. Beatrice was meant to be on her honeymoon right now. That and *no one* called him Jamie.

He'd gone back to James the day she'd left. He'd changed a lot of things since then.

"Jamie, is that you?"

For a moment everything blurred into the background as he looked straight into the eyes of the woman he had once thought he would spend his life with.

Still the same dark, get-lost-in-them irises, but there was something new in them. Something… *wary*. No, that wasn't right. Something…fragile. Unsure. Things he'd never seen in them before.

Her hair was different. Still short, but… Why had she gone platinum? Her formerly chestnut-brown hair, silky soft, particularly when it brushed against… A shot of heat shunted through him as powerfully as it had the first time he'd touched it. Touched *her*.

Instinct took over. She was struggling with a patient. Before he could think better of it, he was on the other side of her, calling to his colleague to find a wheelchair.

"What's your name, love?" he asked the girl, who was whispering words of encouragement to herself in English.

"Leah," Beatrice answered for her. "Leah Stokes."

Jamie hid a flinch as the sound of Beatrice's voice lanced another memory he'd sealed tight. If he'd doubted for a second that this transformed woman—the blond hair, the uncharacteristically plain clothing, the slight shadows hinting at sleepless nights—was the love of his life, he knew it now. She had a husky, made-for-late-night-radio voice that was perfect for a doctor offering words as an immediate antidote for pain. Even better for a lover whispering sweet nothings in your ear.

"The exam table isn't far away. Instead of waiting shall we—" Beatrice began.

He nodded before she'd finished. Once-familiar routines returned to him with an ease he hadn't expected. The looks that made language unnecessary. The gestures the said everything. They'd done this particular move when he'd "popped in" accidentally on purpose to help out with her trauma training. Carried patients here and there. Practiced the weave of wrists and hands. Supported each other.

"On three?" The rush of memory and emotion almost blindsided him. He'd been a fool to let her go. Not to fight harder.

But a modern-day commoner versus a latter-day prince?

There'd been no contest. He'd seen it in her eyes.

Like a fool, he looked up.

"One…two…"

He saw the words appear on her lips but could hardly hear them, such was the rush of blood charging around his head.

Never again.

That was what he'd told himself.

Never again would he let himself be so naive. So vulnerable. So in love.

As one they dipped, eyes glued to each other's, clasped one another's wrists and scooped up the patient between them, hardly feeling Leah's fingers as they pressed into their shoulders once she'd been lifted off the ground.

It definitely wasn't the way he'd imagined seeing Beatrice again. If ever.

"Just here on the exam table, *per favore*." Beatrice had shifted her gaze to her patient, her hands slipping to Leah's leg to ensure the abraded skin was kept clear of rubbing against the paper covering the table. "Thank you, Dr. Coutts."

Her dark brown eyes flitted back toward him before she returned her full attention to her patient, but in that micromoment he saw all that he needed to know. Seeing him had thrown her as off-kilter as it had him.

Whether it was a good thing or a bad thing was impossible to ascertain. At least he hadn't seen the thing he feared most: indifference. He would have packed his bags and left then and there. But something—the tiniest glimmer of something bright flickering in those espresso-rich eyes of hers—said it would be worth his while to stay.

Answers were answers, after all.

"I'll leave you to it, then," he said, tugging the curtain around the exam table, his eyes taking just a fraction of a second longer than necessary to search her hand for the ring. Jewelry had never been his thing, but that ridiculously huge, pink cushion-cut diamond ring—a family heirloom, she'd said—was etched in his mind's eye as clearly as the day she'd told him she was moving back to Italy. *Family*, she'd said. *Obligations. Tradition.*

He yanked the curtain shut, unable to move as he processed what he'd seen. Pleasure? Pain? Satisfaction that neither of them had succeeded in gaining what they'd sought?

A chilling numbness began to creep through his veins.

No sign of a ring.

Nothing.

Each and every one of her fingers was bare.

Bea's heart was thumping so hard behind her simple cotton top she was sure her patient could see it.

Even though she had taken longer than normal to put on her hygienic gloves, Leah would have had to be blind not to notice her fingers shaking.

Jamie Coutts.

The only man who'd laid full claim to her heart.

Why wasn't he in England?

Leaving Jamie had been the most painful thing she'd ever done. The betrayal she'd seen in his eyes would stay with her forever. Having to live with it was so much worse.

"Is everything all right?" Leah asked.

"Si, va bene." Bea gave her head a quick shake, pushed her hands between her knees to steady them and reminded herself to speak English. She had a patient. Rehashing the day she'd told the man she loved she was going to marry another would have to wait.

"Let's take a look at this leg of yours." Bea

gave her hands a quick check. Jitter-free. *Good.* "Cycling, was it?"

"We were coming down one of the passes," Leah confirmed, her wince deepening as Bea began gently to press the blue pads of her gloved hands along the injury. "A car came up alongside me. I panicked and hit the verge too fast."

"A fall when you're wearing these clip shoes can be tough. It looks largely superficial. Not too much bleeding. But from the swelling on your knee it looks like you took quite a blow." Bea glanced up at her, "I'm just going to take your shoes off, all right? Do you feel like anything might be broken? Sprained?"

Leah shook her head. "It's hard to say. I think it's the road rash that hurts the most, but my knee *is* throbbing!"

"Did you get any ice on it straight after you fell? A cool pack?"

"No..." Leah tugged her fingers through her short tangle of hazel curls, loosening some meadow grass as she did so, before swiping at a few more tears. "The guys had all ridden ahead. Downhill pelotons freak me out—and I wasn't carrying a first-aid kit with me. A local couple saw me fall and brought me here."

Poor thing. Left to fend for herself.

It's not any fun, is it, amore?

Bea gave her a smile. "Trying to keep up with a peloton of adrenaline junkies is tough." She pushed herself back on the wheelie stool and looked in the supplies cart for the best dressings. "I don't think you've broken anything, but it's probably worth getting some X-rays just in case."

"But we've still got four more days of riding!" Leah protested, the streaks of dirt on her face disappearing in dark trickles as her tears increased. "Richard's going to think I'm such a weakling. This was meant to be the time I showed him I could keep up with the boys."

Bea took a quick glance at Leah's fingers. Bare, just like hers. "Boyfriend?" she chanced.

"Probably not for long. He's going to think I'm such a wimp!"

"With a road rash like that?" Bea protested with a smile. "This shows *exactly* how tough you are. I've had men in here with half the scraping *your* thigh has taken, howling like babies."

"Howling?" A smile teased at Leah's lips.

"Howling," Bea confirmed with a definitive nod.

She wouldn't mind tipping back her head and letting out a full-pelt she-wolf howl herself right now, but instead she told herself off in her mother's exacting tones. *Princesses don't howl. Princesses set an example.*

She screwed her lips to the right as she forced her attention back to Leah's leg. "*Mi scusi*, I can't see what I need to dress this leg of yours in here. I want to get some alginate and silver dressings for you."

"What are those?"

"They're both pretty amazing, actually. You should get some dressings to carry in your pack. There are derivatives from algae in one of them—really good for wounds like this. Ones that ooze."

Leah sucked in her breath after touching a spot on her thigh. "It's so disgusting."

"It's not pretty now, but it will definitely heal well. Once the dressing gets wet, it will begin to form a gel and absorb any liquid from the abrasion." She pressed her hands into her knees and put on her best I-know-it-stinks face. "Keeping the wound moist is essential to preventing scarring. The dressing I'm hoping to use contains silver. It's antibacterial, so it will keep the wound clean of infection." Bea tipped her head to catch Leah's eye before she rose. "Are you going to be all right for a few minutes while I get the supplies?"

Leah half nodded, her interest already diverted as she pulled her phone out of her bag and flicked on the camera app. "I'm going to send the guys some pictures. Give them a proper guilt trip for abandoning me."

"Back in a minute," Bea said unnecessarily as Leah snapped away.

No doubt the photos would be hitting all sorts of social media sites in seconds. She'd taken all those things off her *telefono* within hours of the wedding being called off. She'd even tried throwing the phone in a canal when some wily reporter had got hold of her number, but Francesca hadn't let her.

"Just put the thing on Mute or change your number," Fran had insisted. "*Use* us. Stay contactable. We want to help."

If only someone *could* help. But she and she alone had got herself into this mess.

Bea hurried into the supplies room before a fresh hit of tears glossed her eyes. She missed her best friend. Could really do with a Bea-and-Fran night on the sofa. A pizza. Box set. Bottle of wine—nope! Nix the wine. But… Oh…nix everything. Now that Fran had gone and fallen in love with Luca, and the pair of them were making a real go of the clinic at Mont di Mare, Bea would have to make do on her own. And stay busy. Extra busy. Any and all distractions were welcome.

She forced herself to focus on the shelves of supplies, desperate to remember why she'd gone to the room in the first place.

"Hello, Beatrice."

She froze at the sound of Jamie's voice. Then, despite every single one of her senses being on high alert, she smiled. How could she have forgotten it? That Northern English lilt of his accent. The liquid edge he added to the end of her name where Italians turned it into two harsher syllables. From his tongue her named sounded like sweet mountain water…

When she turned to face him, her smile dropped instantly. Jamie's expression told her everything she needed to know.

He wasn't letting bygones stay back in England, where she'd left him some seven-hundred-odd days ago. But who was counting? Numbers meant nothing when everything about his demeanor told her it was the witching hour. Time to confront the past she'd never been able to forget.

"Since when does Italy's most pampered princess get her own supplies?"

The comment held more rancor than Jamie had hoped to achieve. He'd been aiming for a casual "fancy meeting you here," but he'd actually nailed expressing the months of bitterness he'd been unable to shake since she'd left him. True, he hadn't put up much of a fight, but she had made it more than clear that her future was in Italy. With another man.

It had blindsided him. One minute they were more in love than he could imagine a couple ever being. The next, after that sudden solo trip to Venice, her heart had belonged to another.

He'd not thought her so fickle. It had been a harsh way to learn why they called love blind.

When their gazes connected the color dropped from Beatrice's face. A part of him hated eliciting this bleak reaction—another part was pleased to see he still had an effect on her.

Ashen faced with shaking palms wasn't what he'd been hoping for… Seeing her *at all* hadn't been what he'd been hoping for…but no matter how hard he tried, no matter how many corners he'd turned since he'd left England, he didn't seem to be able to shake her. This was either kismet or some sort of hellish purgatory. From the look on her face, it wasn't the former.

Self-loathing swept through him for lashing out at Beatrice. A woman who'd done little more than proactively pursue the life she wanted. Which was more than he could say for himself.

"What are you doing here, Beatrice? Aren't you meant to be on honeymoon? Or is this part of it? Dropping in to local clinics to grace us with your largesse before embarking on a shopping spree. Dubai, perhaps? Turkey? Shouldn't you be buying silver spoons for the long line of di Jesolos yet to come into the world?"

Jamie hated himself as the vitriol poured out of him. Hated himself even more as he watched Beatrice's full lips part only to say nothing, her features crumpling in disbelief as if he'd shivved her right then and there rather than simply pointed out everything the tabloids had been crowing about. The engagement. The impending wedding. The royal babies they were hoping would quickly follow the exotic and lengthy honeymoon.

A month ago he'd refused to read anymore. He'd endured enough.

He looked deep into her eyes, willing her to tell him something. Anything to ease the pain.

As quickly as the ire had flared up in him, it disappeared.

You're not this man. She must've had her reasons.

Jamie took a step forward, his natural instinct to put a hand on Beatrice's arm—to touch her, to apologize. As he closed the space between them the handful of gel packs and silver dressings she'd been holding dropped from her fingers. They knelt simultaneously to collect them, colliding with the inevitable head bump and mumbled apologies.

Crouching on the floor, each with a hand to their forehead, they stared at one another as if waiting for the other to pounce.

By God, she is beautiful.

"You've grown your hair," she said finally.

She was so close he could kiss her. Put his hand at the nape of her neck as he'd done so many times before, draw her to him and…

She was talking about haircuts.

A haircut had been the last thing on his mind when she'd left. *Work.* Work had been all he'd had and he'd thrown himself so far into the deep end he'd been blind to everything else. Got too involved. So close he'd literally drained the blood from his own body to help ease the pain of his patient.

Elisa.

That poor little girl. They'd shared a rare blood type. Foolishly he'd thought that if he saved her life he might be able to save himself. In the end his boss had made him choose. Take a step back or leave.

So here he was in Italy, just when he'd thought

he was beginning to see straight again, eye to eye with the woman who had all but sucked the marrow from his bones.

"It looks nice," Beatrice said, her finger indicating the hair he knew curled on and around his shirt collar. What was it she'd always called him? Hay head? Straw head? Something like that. Something that brought back too many memories of those perfect summer months they'd shared together.

He nodded his thanks. Blissful summers were a thing of the past. Now they were reduced to social niceties.

Fair enough. He glanced at his watch. The chopper would be leaving in five. He needed to press on.

"C'mon. Let's get these picked up. Get you back to your patient." No matter how deeply he'd been hurt, patients were the priority.

She reached forward, sucking in a sharp breath when their fingers brushed, each reaching for the same packet of dressings.

"I'm not made of poison, you know."

Beatrice's gaze shot up to meet his, those rich brown eyes of hers looking larger than ever. He couldn't tell if it was because she'd lost weight or because they were punctuated by twilight-blue shadows. Either way, she didn't look happy.

"No one knows who I am here," she bit out, her voice low and urgent as she clutched the supplies to her chest. "I would appreciate it if you could keep it that way."

A huff of disbelief emptied his chest of oxygen. Flaunting the family name was the reason she'd left him, and now she wanted to be *anonymous*?

She met his gaze as she finished scanning his uniform. "Since when do pediatricians wear high-octane rescue gear? I thought life in a children's ward was all the excitement you needed?"

"Snide comments were never your thing."

"Pushing boundaries was never *yours*."

Jamie's lungs strained against a deep breath, all the while keeping tight hold of the eye contact. He wanted her to see the man he'd become.

After a measured exhalation he let himself savor the pain of his teeth grating across his lower lip. He turned to leave, then changed his mind, throwing the words over his shoulder as if it were the most casual thing in the world to lacerate the woman he loved with words.

"People change, Dr. Jesolo. Some of us for the better."

Ten minutes later and the sting of his comment still hadn't worn off. Perhaps it never would.

And hiding in the staff room with her friendly Aussie colleague had only made things worse. He was a messenger with even more bad news.

Jamie Coutts was not just back in her life—he was her boss.

"Wait a minute, Teo." Bea held up a hand, hardly believing what she was hearing. "He's *what*?"

Teo Brandisi gave Bea a patient smile and handed her the cup of herbal tea he'd promised her hours earlier in the busy shift.

"The big boss man. The big kahuna. Mayor of medics."

"But *you* hired me."

"He was out in the field. He hands over the reins to me when he's away."

"But—"

"Quit trying to fight it, sweetheart. He's *le*

grand fromage—all right? I wouldn't be working here without his approval, so if you've got a bone to pick with him, I'm recusing myself. He has my back. I have his. You got me?" Teo continued in his broad Australian accent.

Bea shook her head and waved her hands. "No, it's not that. I've nothing *against* Dr. Coutts."

Liar.

She cleared her throat, forcing herself to sound more neutral. "I just don't understand why he had to approve appointing *you* but not me."

"Foreign doctor." Teo pointed at himself. "We can't just swan in and take all the choice jobs. Even though he's English, he's been qualified to practice here for over a year."

He'd been in Italy for a year and she hadn't known.

Well…she'd done a whole lot of things *he* didn't know about, so fair was fair.

"My advice?" Teo was on a roll. "You have to suck up to people like James Coutts."

"James?"

"Yeah… Why?"

Teo scrunched up his nose and looked at her as if she was giving proof positive she was losing her marbles. Maybe she was. And if Jamie was James, and she'd shortened her name to Bea, then the only thing that was clear was that they were both trying to be someone new.

A reinvention game.

Only games were meant to be fun. And everything about seeing Jamie again was far from fun. Confronting what she'd done to him was going to be the hardest thing she'd ever done.

"Anyhoo..." Teo continued. "James has got the whole British-reserve thing going on big-time." A glint of admiration brightened his blue eyes. "The man's like an impenetrable fortress. Impossible to read. Well done!" He clapped her on the shoulder. "A gold star to Dr. Jesolo for getting under the Stone Man's skin!"

"The Stone Man?"

"Yeah. We all take bets on how many facial expressions he actually has. I'm going with three. Contemplative. Not happy. And his usual go-to face—Mr. Neutral. No reading that face. No way, no how."

Bea hid her face in the steam of her tea for a minute. Her kind, gentle Jamie was an impenetrable fortress? That wasn't like him. Then again…*she* was hardly the same. Why should *he* be?

"It's most likely a fluke. That or he doesn't like blondes?"

Teo gave her a sidelong glance as if he already knew the whole story. Could tell she was just making things up. Covering a truth she wasn't yet ready to divulge.

"Fair enough."

They stood in an awkward silence until Bea launched into a sudden interest in removing her herbal tea bag from her mug.

If Teo had known she was pregnant, she could have just blown the whole thing off as a bout of pregnancy brain. Not that she even knew if pregnancy brain hit this early. Sharp bouts of fatigue certainly had. And morning sickness. She'd never look at a hamburger the same way again! At least when she'd been on her brother's yacht she'd managed to fob off the nausea she'd felt as seasickness. Now that she was up here in the mountains she couldn't do that. It was meant to pass soon. And by the time her contract was up she'd be off to hide away the rest of her pregnancy somewhere else.

"So, on a day-to-day basis *you're* my boss?" She kept her eyes on her tea, wincing at the note of hope in her voice.

"Nope. Dr. James Coutts is your actual boss," Teo continued, after taking his shot of espresso down in one swift gulp.

Classic Italian. She would be amazed if he went back to Australia. He might be second generation in Australia, but the man had Italy in his bones.

"I step in when he's out on rescue calls, like today. The fact I was on duty when we held your interview was just a coincidence."

"So…he knew I was coming?"

The interview had been a week ago. Start date today. He'd had a whole week to come to terms with things and yet she was sure she'd seen shock in his eyes. The same shock of recognition that had reverberated through to her very core.

"He knew *someone* was coming, but he's been tied up training the emergency squads."

Her Jamie? Better-safe-than-sorry Jamie?

She'd always thought *she* was a solid rock until

she'd met him. But no one had been more reliable, more sound than him.

"He's pretty good about not breathing down your neck." Teo pulled open a cupboard and began to look around for some biscuits. "And he lets staff make decisions in his absence. He's a really good guy, actually. Don't let the whole Dr. Impenetrable thing get to you."

Her lips thinned. Jamie was better than a good guy. He was the kindest man she'd ever met.

Strangely, it came as a relief to hear his bitterness seemed to be solely reserved for her. Deservedly so. How she could have dumped him just to make good on an antiquated match between her family and the Roldolfos was beyond her now. Family loyalty meant altogether different things when your blue-blooded mother was trying to uphold hundreds of years of tradition. Pass the princess baton…even if it came at her daughter's expense.

She heard Teo sigh and looked up to catch him lovingly gazing at a plate of homemade biscotti. Someone's grandmother's, no doubt. There was a lot of bragging about grandmothers up here. She missed hers. No doubt *she* would have had some wise words for the insane situation Bea was in now.

"Did you hear the crew earlier? Sounds like it was a pretty intense case," Teo continued, oblivious to the turmoil Bea was enduring.

"I didn't see any patients come down from the helipad." She shook her head in confusion.

"They dropped the patient off in Switzerland. A little kid. Five, maybe six years old—broke his leg. Compound fracture. Tib-fib job. Massive blood loss. The mother nearly lost the plot. She was attacking the staff, threatened to kill one of them if they didn't let her on the helicopt—"

"All right, all right." Bea held up a hand, feeling a swell of nausea rise and take hold as he painted the picture. "It's obvious someone's a bit jealous that *he* wasn't out on the rescue squad today."

"I'm on tomorrow." Teo gave his hands a quick excited rub. "You can sign up, too, if you like. We do it on rotation, because summers are so busy up here, but you'd probably have to do your first few with James. The man is a right daredevil when's he's wearing the old rescue gear.

Biscotti?" He held out a plate filled with the oblong biscuits.

"*No, grazie.* Or, actually..." Maybe it would help settle her stomach. She took one of the crunchy biscuits and gave him a smile.

He gave the door frame a final pat and then was gone.

Bea sank into a nearby chair. As far as she was concerned, Teo could have all her emergency-rescue shifts. About eight weeks, two days and... she glanced at her watch...three hours ago she would have been all over them. High-octane rescues and first-class medical treatment? *Amazing* experiences.

Experiences she would have to miss now.

Compromising the tiny life inside her while the former love of her life looked on...

She let her head sink into her hands.

Clinica Torpisi wasn't going to be the healing hideaway she'd been hoping for.

More like hell on earth.

CHAPTER TWO

HE SAW HER across the piazza. Jamie wondered now, having adjusted to the platinum blond hair, how he hadn't noticed her instantly. He certainly had when she'd walked into Northern General. How could he not have when he'd entered the *clinica*?

Fathomless chocolate-brown eyes straight out of the Italian-nymph guidebook. Slender. The darkest chestnut hair he'd ever seen. Short, but thick enough to lose his hands in when he wanted to put his fingers against the nape of her soft, swan-like neck. Perfect raspberry-red lips. Olive skin. Carrying herself like royalty.

She was royalty.

He shook his head again.

Little wonder he hadn't recognized her straight off. He hadn't wanted to.

A bit of shock.

A splash of denial.

Hope, pain, love, despair… All those things and more made up the roiling ball of conflict burning in his heart. Most of all he just wanted to understand *why*.

He hitched his trousers onto his hips. She wasn't the only one who'd lost weight in the past couple of years.

Stop apportioning blame.

The closer he got, the more he wondered what the hell he was doing.

No. That wasn't true. Ripping off the bandage had become his modus operandi since she'd left. He might as well stick true to his course. Life wasn't sweet. Might as well get used to it.

"Mind if I join you?"

Beatrice started, as if her thoughts had been a thousand miles away. When she'd pulled him into focus he watched as she searched his face for signs of enmity. He couldn't say he blamed her. After his performance in the supplies room earlier in the day he'd hardly made a good show of the manners his mother had drilled into him.

"Please…" Beatrice pushed aside a small plate of antipasti and indicated the chair beside her. One from which he could enjoy the stunning lakeside view. One that would seat them side by side, where they wouldn't have to look into the other's eyes.

He sank into the chair, grateful for this reprieve from animosity. Perhaps a few hours apart had been what they'd each needed. Time to process.

"Is that a spritzer you're having?" He pointed at the bright orange drink on the table, the glass beaded with condensation as the final rays of sunlight disappeared behind the mountain peaks beyond the lake.

"No." She shook her head. "I never liked spritzers. Too..." Her nose crinkled as she sought the right word. "Aftertasty," she said finally, her lips tipping up into the first suggestion of a smile he'd seen. "Orange soda is my new guilty pleasure. I don't seem to be able to drink enough of it."

He was about to launch into the lecture he gave all his patients—too many fizzy drinks were bad for the bones, bad for the brain, bad for the body—but just seeing the tension release from the corners of her eyes as she lifted the glass, put her lips around the red and white stripes of the straw and drew in a cool draught made him swallow it.

He hadn't come here to deliver a lecture. He had questions. Thousands of questions.

A waiter swooped in, as they all did at this time of day, keen to get as many people as possible their drinks before the early-dining Americans began infiltrating the wide square in advance of the Europeans.

He and Beatrice both bit back smiles at the waiter's terse "Is that all for *signor*?" after he'd settled on a sparkling water.

"Going back to the clinic?" Beatrice asked.

"That obvious?"

"Mmm, 'fraid so." Beatrice looked out toward the square as she spoke. "It would be a glass of Gavi di Gavi if you were finished, wouldn't it? If…" She hesitated. "If memory serves me right."

He nodded. Surprised she'd remembered such a silly detail. Then again, there wasn't a single detail he'd forgotten about *her*. Maybe…

He rammed his knuckles into his thigh.

Maybe was for other people. He was all about sure things. And Beatrice wasn't one of them.

Jamie scrubbed a hand along his chin, then scraped his chair around on the stone cobbles until he faced her head-on.

"What are you doing here, Beatrice?"

"Well, that's a nice way to—" She stopped herself and lifted a hand so that he would give her a moment to think. Say what she really meant to.

Despite himself, he smiled. She'd always been that way. A thinker. Just like him. The more they'd learned about each other, the stronger the pull had been. Interns hadn't been meant to date residents—but try telling that to two people drawn to each other as magnetically as iron and nitrogen. Weighted and weightless. He'd felt both of those things when he'd been with her. Secure in himself as he'd never been before, and so damn happy he would have sworn his feet hadn't touched the ground after the first time he'd tasted those raspberry-ripe lips of hers.

"You *have* read the papers lately, haven't you?" Beatrice asked eventually.

"I have a hunch that world peace is a long way off, so I tend to steer clear of them." Jamie leant forward in his chair, elbows pressed to his knees.

"C'mon, Beatrice. Quit throwing questions back at me. Why are you in Torpisi?"

She shook her head in disbelief. "You are the one person in the world I wish had read the tabloids and you *haven't*!" She threw her hands up in the air and gave a small isn't-the-world-ridiculous? laugh.

When their eyes met again there was kindness in hers. A tenderness reserved just for him that he might have lived on in a different time and place.

"I never got married."

She took another sip of her soft drink and looked away as casually as if she'd just told him the time. Or perhaps it was guilt that wouldn't let her meet his eye.

Jamie blinked a few times, his body utterly stationary, doing its best to ingest the news.

Despite his best efforts to remain neutral, something hardened in him. "Is this some sort of joke?"

She shook her head, seemingly confused about the question.

"Why did you do it?"

"Do what?" It was her turn to look bewildered.

"Oh, well…let's see, here, love. Quite a few things, now that I come to think of it."

He spread out his fingers and started ticking them off, his tone level, though his message was heated.

"Up and leave me for a man you didn't love. Ruin the future we'd planned together. All that to never even see it through?"

He pulled his fingers into tight fists and gave his thighs a quick drumming.

"Is this some sort of cruel game you're playing, Beatrice?"

He pushed back in his chair and rose, no longer sure he could even look her in the eye.

"If you're here to rub it in and make sure you made your impact, you can count me *out*."

"Jamie! Wait!"

Bea's voice sounded harsh to her own ears. As quickly as she'd reached out to stop Jamie from leaving she wished she'd rescinded the invitation, tightly wrapping her arms around herself to brace herself against the shards of ice coursing through her veins.

She'd betrayed too much by calling out to him.

Jamie would know better than anyone that there had been pain in her voice. The ache of loss. But what was she going to do? Explain what a fool she'd been? That she'd gone and got herself pregnant at an IVF clinic in advance of her wedding so her family, the press and the whole of Italy could coo and smile over the Prince and the Principessa's "honeymoon baby"?

She was the only one in the world who knew that her fiancé—her *ex*-fiancé—was infertile, apart from a doctor whose silence had been bought. She was surprised he'd even told *her*. Perhaps their family get-togethers had begun to rely a bit too heavily on talk of children running around the palazzo, in order to cover up the obvious fact that neither of them were very much in love.

Their one joint decision: an IVF baby. Keeping it as quiet as possible. A private clinic. More paid-off doctors and nurses. An anonymous donor.

The less anyone knew, the easier it had been to go ahead with it.

Her sole investment in a relationship she had known would never claim her heart. A child…

A child who had been meant to bring some light into her life.

Now it just filled her with fear. Confirmation that she'd been a fool to agree to the plan. She no longer had the support of her family and, worse, she would be a single mother in a world where it was already tough enough to survive on her own.

It hadn't felt that way when she'd been with Jamie. With him she'd felt…*invincible.*

Relief washed through her when Jamie sat down again, pressing his hips deeper into the chair, his back ramrod straight as he drained his water glass in one fluid draught before deigning to look her in the eye.

"I'm in trouble, Jamie."

As quickly as he'd tried to leave, Jamie pulled his chair up close, knees wide so they flanked hers, fingers spread as he cupped her face in both his broad hands, searching her eyes for information.

"Are you hurt? Did he hurt you?"

No, but I *hurt you.*

He used an index finger to swipe at a couple of errant locks of hair so his access to her eyes was unfettered. Against his better judgment—she could see that in his eyes—he traced his finger along the contour of her jawline, coming to a halt, as he had so many times before, before gently cradling the length of her neck as if he were about to lean in and kiss her.

It was like rediscovering her senses all over again. As if part of her had died the day she'd told him she was returning home to marry another man.

She blinked away the rising swell of tears.

Part of her *had* died that day. The part that believed in love conquering all. The part that believed in destiny.

"Beatrice," Jamie pressed. "Did he hurt you?"

I was a fool to have left you.

She shook her head, instantly feeling the loss of his touch when he dropped his hands, sat back in his chair and rammed them into his front pockets, as if trying to hide the fact that his long surgeon's fingers were balled into tight fists. For the second time in as many minutes. Twice as many times as she'd ever seen him make the gesture before.

He'd aged in the years since she'd seen him

last. Nothing severe, as if he'd been sick or a decade had passed, but he *had* changed. His was a proper grown-up male face now, instead of holding the hints of youth she had sometimes seen at the hospital, when he'd caught her looking at him and smiled.

It felt like a million years ago. Hard to believe it was just two short years since he'd been thirty-three and she twenty-eight.

"Just a young lass, you are," he would say, and laugh whenever she whined about feeling old after a long shift. "Perfect for me," he'd say, before dropping a surreptitious kiss on her forehead in one of the busy hospital corridors. They'd been little moments in heaven. *Perfect.*

She closed her eyes against the memory, gave them a rub, then forced herself to confront the present. It was all of her own making, so she might as well see it for what it was. *Payback.*

A painful price she knew she had to pay when all she really wanted was for him to love her again as he once had.

Impossible.

Sun-tanned crinkles fanned out from Jamie's eyes, which she still wasn't quite brave enough to meet. The straw gold of his hair was interwoven with a few threads of silver. At the temples, mostly. More than she thought a man of thirty-five should have.

But what would she know? When she grew her dyed hair out again it might *all* be gray after the level of stress she'd endured these past few weeks. It was a wonder she hadn't lost the baby.

Her hands automatically crept to her stomach, one folding protectively over the other.

"Did he *hurt* you?" Jamie repeated, the air between them thick with untold truths.

"Only my pride," she conceded. "He didn't want me."

The explanation came out as false, too chirpy. She hadn't wanted Marco either. What she most likely really owed him was a thank-you letter.

"Can you believe it?" She put on a smile and grinned at the real love of her life, as if having her arranged marriage grind to a halt in front of some of Europe's most elite families had been the silliest thing to have happened to her in years.

"He should be shot."

"Jamie..." Bea shook her head. "Don't be—"

She huffed out a lungful of frustration, then unfolded her arms from their tight cinch across her chest, visible proof she was trying her best to be honest with him. Open. Vulnerable. "*Mi scusi.* I'm sorry. I don't have any right to tell you what to feel."

"You're damn right you don't," he shot back, but with less venom than before.

Something in her gave. He deserved to vent whatever amount of spleen he needed to.

"Serves you right" was probably lurking there in his throat. Along with a bit of "now you know how it feels" followed by a splash of "what goes around comes around" as a chaser.

She deserved the venom—and more.

After a moment had passed, with each of them silently collecting their thoughts, Jamie reached across and took one of her hands in his, weaving their fingers together as naturally as if they'd never been apart.

A million tiny sparks lit up inside her. A sensation she'd never once felt with her ex-fiancé.

Obligation didn't elicit rushes of desire. She'd learned that the hard way.

"Talk to me, Beatrice."

His voice was gentle. Kind. His thumb rubbed along the back of her hand as his features softened, making it clear he was present—there just for her.

In that instant she felt he was back. The man she'd met and fallen in love with in the corridors of a busy inner-city hospital tucked way up in the North of England. Their entire worlds had been each other and medicine.

She vividly remembered the first time she'd seen him. So English! *Male.* He'd exuded...*capability.* So refreshing after a lifetime of worrying about etiquette and decorum and the thousands of other silly little things that had mattered to her mother and not one jot to her. Surviving finishing school had been down to Fran. Without her... She didn't even want to think about it.

She glanced up at Jamie. His eyes were steady...patient... She knew as well as he did that he would wait all evening if he needed to.

She lifted her gaze just in time to see the topmost arc of the sun disappear behind the mountain peaks.

"Maybe we could walk?" she suggested.

He nodded, unlacing his fingers from hers as he rose.

She curled one hand around the other in a ridiculous attempt to save the sensation.

He pointed toward the far end of the piazza. "Let's go out along the lake. Have you been to the promenade yet? Seen the boats?"

She shook her head. She'd had enough of boats and morning sickness over the past few weeks to last a lifetime. She agreed to the route anyway. It wasn't as if this was meant to be *easy*.

Every part of Jamie itched to reach out and touch Beatrice. Hold her hand. Put a protective arm around her shoulder. There was something incredibly fragile about her he wasn't sure he'd seen before. She was nursing something more than a chink in her pride. And all the rage he'd thought would come to the fore if he ever found himself in her orbit again… It was there, all right. It just wasn't ready to blow.

Instinct told him to take things slowly. And then start digging. A verbal attack would elicit nothing. As for a physical attack… If that man had laid one finger on her—

"How are you settling in here? Everyone at the clinic helping you get your bearings?"

Beatrice nodded enthusiastically. "I love it. All one day of it, that is."

He smiled at the note of genuine happiness in her voice. Excellent. The staff were making her feel at home. He fought the need to press her. To get her to spill everything. Explain how she'd found it so easy to break his heart.

"Your contract is…?"

"For the rest of the summer. I guess one of the early-summer staffers left before expected?"

"No." He shook his head. "She had a baby. Worked right up until her due date."

"Ah…"

Beatrice's gaze jumped from boat to boat moored along the quayside. Families and groups of friends were spilling out onto the promenade to find which restaurant they'd eat in tonight.

"I suppose she'll be coming back, then, after maternity leave. Although I did tell your colleague, Dr. Brandisi, that I would be happy to extend if the clinic loses any essential staff after the season ends."

"It waxes and wanes up here. There'll be a

time when the summer wraps up where we hit a lull, and then ski season brings in another lot. It's usually all right with just the bare minimum of hands on deck."

Beatrice threw a quick smile his way, her lips still pressed tight, so he continued. "Mostly Italians to start, then Swiss, German, Austrian… A complete pick 'n' mix at the height of the season."

That was why he liked it. Nothing stayed the same. Change was the only thing keeping him afloat since he'd finally faced facts and left Northern General. Everything about that place had reminded him of Beatrice. And then, after Elisa… That had been the hardest time of death he'd ever had to call.

He swallowed and pushed his finger through a small pool of lake water on the square guard railing, visibly dividing it in two.

Everything leaves its mark. And nothing stays the same.

Those were the two lessons he'd learned after Beatrice had left. Now was the time to prove it.

He rubbed his hands together and belatedly returned her smile. "So! What sort of cases have you had today? Anything juicy?"

They might as well play My Injuries Were Worse Than Yours until she was ready to talk.

The tension in Beatrice's shoulders eased and she relaxed into a proper smile. "Actually, all my cases have been really different to what I treated at home in Venice. With all the recreational sports up here I'm seeing all sorts of new things. It's made a great change."

He felt his jaw shift at the mention of "home." Home—for a few months at the end of their relationship, at least—had been their tiny little apartment, around the corner from the hospital. The one they'd vowed to stay in until they could afford one of the big, rambling stone homes on the outer reaches of the city. One of those houses that would fall apart if someone didn't give it some TLC. The kind of house where there'd be plenty of room for children to play. Not that they'd talked about the two boys and two girls they'd hoped to have one day. *Much.*

Let it go, Jamie. It was all just a pipe dream.

"Were you still working in trauma? When you came back to Italy?" he added.

"Off and on." She nodded. "But mostly I was working in a free clinic for refugees. So many people coming in on boats..."

"With all your language skills you must've been a real asset. Were you based in Venice?" He might as well try to visualize some sort of picture.

"Just outside. On the mainland." She stopped farther along the railing, where the view to the lake and the mountains beyond was unimpeded by boats, and drew in a deep breath, curling her fingers around the cool metal until her knuckles were pale.

The deepening colors of the early-evening sky rendered the lake a dark blue—so dark it was hard to imagine how deep it might be. Fathomless.

"It was relentless. Working there. The poverty. The sickness. The number of lives lost all in the pursuit of a dream."

"Happiness?" he asked softly.

"Freedom."

When she turned to him the hit of connection was so powerful he almost stumbled. It was as if she was trying to tell him something. That her moving back to Italy had been a mistake? That she wished she could turn back time as much as he did?

"Do you miss it? Working at the refugee clinic?" he qualified.

If she was going to up and leave again, he had to know. Had to reassemble the wall he'd been building brick by brick around his heart only to have the foundations crumble to bits when she'd walked back into his life.

She turned her head, resting her chin on her shoulder, and looked at him.

"No." Her head shook a little. "I mean, it was obviously rewarding. But I don't miss being there. Venice…"

Something in him gave. His breath began filling his lungs a bit more deeply.

"What drew you up here to our little Alpine retreat?"

He leant against the railing, unsurprised to see her give him a sideways double take.

Nice one, Jamie. Super casual. Not.

"I used to come up here to one of my cousins' places. Skiing. The next valley over, actually," she corrected herself, then continued, her eyes softening into a faraway smile. "One year I brought Fran with me. Remember Francesca? My mad friend from America? I don't think you met her, but she was—" Beatrice stopped, the smile dropping from her eyes. "We saw each other recently. She's getting married."

"Ah." Jamie nodded.

What was he meant to say to that? *Congratulations, I wish I was, too?* He elbowed the rancorous thoughts away and reharnessed himself to the light-banter variety of conversational tactics.

"Wasn't there something about finishing school and a giggle-laden walk of shame before the term was out? Mussed-up white gloves or something?"

"We snuck away one day." Beatrice feigned a gasp of horror. "Away from the 'good' set."

"You mean the 'crowned cotillion crowd'?" he asked without thinking twice.

Beatrice had been so contemptuous of them then. The group of titled friends and extended family who seemed to drift across Europe together in packs. Hunting down the next in place, the next big thing so they could put their mark on it, suck it dry, then leave. The exact type of person she'd left him for. *Oh, the irony.*

When he looked across to see if his comment had rankled he was surprised to see another small cynical smile in Beatrice's dark eyes.

Huh. Maybe she'd softened. Saw things now she hadn't before. Not that he and Beatrice had ever "hung with the crowd." Nor any crowd, for that matter. They had been a self-contained unit.

It had never once occurred to him that she was keeping him at arm's length from the affluent, titled set she'd grown up with. He'd never considered himself hung up on his low-income upbringing. The opposite, if anything. Proud. He was from a typical Northern family. Typical of his part of the North anyway. Father down the mines. Mother working as a dinner lady at the local primary school. Brother and sister had followed suit, but he'd been the so-called golden boy. Scholarships to private schools. Oxford University. An internship at London's most prestigious pediatric hospital before he'd returned to the part of the country he'd always called home.

Meeting and falling in love with Beatrice had just been part of the trajectory. *Local boy falls in love with princess.* Only that hadn't been the way it had played out at all. He hadn't known about Beatrice's past for—had it been a year? Maybe longer. Those two years at Northern General had been like living in a cocoon. Nestled up there in the part of the country he knew and loved best, hoping he'd spend each and every day of the rest of his life with Beatrice by his side.

He cleared his throat. "Sorry—you were saying about your friend?"

"*Si*—yes." Bea gave her head a shake, as if clearing away her own memories. "She's staying in Italy. Fallen in love with an Italian."

"Happens to the best of us."

Beatrice looked away.

He hadn't meant to say that. Not in that way. Not with anger lacing the words.

"It's a magical place up here. I'm glad I came," she said at last.

He nodded, turning to face the view. Despite the summer, snow still capped the high Alpine ridges soaring above the broad expanse of blue that was one of Europe's most beautiful high-altitude lakes.

"You know there's a little island out there?"

"Really? Uninhabited?"

"Quite the opposite. There's a group of monks. A small group living there… It's quite a beautiful retreat. Stone and wood. Simple rooms. Cells, they call them."

"Sounds more like a prison than a place of worship." Beatrice's eyebrows tugged together, but her expression was more curious than judgmental.

"No. The simplicity is its beauty. Gives you plenty of time to think."

He should know. He'd spent long enough in one of those cells, just staring at the stone walls until he could find a way to make sense of the world again. The friary was the reason he'd chosen to come here in the first place. He'd needed to hide away from the world for a while and atone for—he still didn't know what.

Failing himself?

Not fighting hard enough for Elisa's life?

Not fighting hard enough for Beatrice?

Those two years they'd spent together in England felt like a lifetime ago. He'd felt…*vital*—full of the joys of life. In his prime. When she'd told him she didn't want him anymore he'd just shut down. "Fine," he had said, and pointed toward the door. *What are you waiting for?*

He sure as hell hadn't found any answers when she'd taken him up on his offer.

And he was certain there hadn't been any when Elisa had died.

He'd found a modicum of peace when he'd gone out to that tiny island friary.

When one of the monks had fallen ill he'd brought him to the clinic here on the lakeside, had accepted the odd shift and found himself, bit by bit, coming back to life. Part of him wondered if the monk had been faking it. And when the clinic "just happened" to mention they needed full-time staff he'd thrown his hat into the ring. He'd been there almost a year now and—as strange as it sounded for a village several hundreds of years old—he felt a part of the place.

"They make some sort of famous Christmas cake—a special sort of panettone. I'm surprised you haven't heard of it."

"The Friars of Torpisi!" Beatrice clapped her hands together, her eyes lighting up as the dots connected. "Of *course*. I had some last *Natale*."

Again that faraway look stole across her face.

What happened to you, my love?

Jamie scrubbed a hand through his hair before stuffing both hands into his pockets again.

Perhaps some questions were best left unanswered.

CHAPTER THREE

"How can you do that?" Bea asked, finally pressing herself into the entire point of the walk. Laying her cards on the table.

"Do what?"

Jamie glanced over at her, his green eyes actively searching her face while the rest of his body remained turned toward the lake.

"Be so forgiving."

"I hardly think I'm being *forgiving*. We've got to work together. It'd be a shame to lose a good doctor because of water under the bridge."

Jamie's hands disappeared behind his back. Whether he was crossing his fingers to cover the lie or polishing a fist to take it out on a wall later, she didn't know. Either way it was a hard hit to take.

Water under the bridge.

No chance of reconciliation. Not that she had

done a single solitary thing to earn his love, much less earn it a second time.

Even so…would it be crazy to take it as an olive branch?

"So you're not going to fire me?"

He looked at her as if she'd gone mad. "Is that what you think this is about? I may be a lot of things, but I'm hardly a sadist, my love."

A surprised laugh escaped her throat. "I can think of a thousand other things you could call me besides—" She stopped, finding herself completely unable to repeat the words.

My love.

A thousand times she'd said them once. More. An infinity of moments she'd closed down all in the name of tradition.

"Why aren't you married?"

Shocked at the bluntness of his question, Bea froze as her mind raced for the right answer. The truth might push him away even further. Yank back his olive branch.

Just tell him. You owe him that much.

"The most immediate answer is that he was cheating on me."

Color flooded Jamie's face. The show of emotion meant more to her than she could say.

She continued before she could think better of it. "So I gave him back his ring and told him the wedding was off."

Jamie's shoulders broadened as he pressed himself to his full height. "He'd better have left the country if he knows what's good for him."

"He has." She had to laugh. "He's taken his new lover on *our* honeymoon."

"The tabloids must be loving that."

Jamie laughed, too, but she could see he was far from amused.

"I've been doing my best to avoid the tabloids."

"Probably just as well."

"Why? Have you heard something?"

"No, no." He held up his hands. "I hate those things as much as you do. They're…*toxic*."

"You've got that right."

He leant against the railing, his back to the view, and folded his arms across his chest. "You don't seem that upset for someone whose fiancé has ripped her future into tatters."

It's so much more complicated than I ever imagined it would be.

"I think you and I both know I never loved him."

There it was. The real truth. Whether or not it would make Jamie hate her more, or ultimately find a way to forgive her, only time would tell.

Jamie's jaw set hard. Long enough for her to wish she'd never said anything. Maybe it would have been better to pretend her ex had broken her heart. That there had been more of a reason than family obligation to her agreeing to the ridiculous marriage.

"Well, that's something anyway," Jamie said, holding his stance. Body taut, shoulders held back. He'd never hunched. Never shied away from anything.

Bea ran a finger along the railing, buying herself a bit of time before being truly honest. "For as long as I can remember my family and his were…were sort of *promised* to one another."

"The families, or you and their son?"

"Me and their son," she confirmed.

It sounded so clinical. Patriarchal. Hierarchal. Archaic. You name it. But that was what it had been. An arranged marriage cloaked in a foolish whirlwind of cocktail parties, whispered promises she'd hardly let herself believe—thank heavens—and her mother's long-sought joy. Her satisfaction that, finally, her daughter was behaving like a proper princess.

In other words, she'd taken one for the team.

"Your mother never really liked it that you came to England, did she? Worked in the A&E."

"Have you added mind reading to your skills list since I saw you last?"

Without even thinking about it she reached across and gave his forearm a squeeze. They'd always been like that. Touching one another. Confirming each cue—verbal or social—with a little hug, a little stroke on the cheek, a light brush of the fingers as they passed in a corridor too populated for them to get away with a proper kiss.

Jamie looked down, considered her hand for a minute, then looked back up into her eyes. "I always used to think I could read your mind, but after you left… Not so much."

She dropped her hand back to her side. "I could've handled that better."

"You could have stayed."

Tears leapt to her eyes, and for the first time

since she'd laid eyes on him, Jamie didn't do a thing. No pad of his thumb wiping them away. No digging into one of his pockets for a fresh linen handkerchief. Just the set of his jaw growing tighter.

She *should* have stayed. Been true to her heart *and* his. Then she wouldn't be in this ludicrous position. Unmarried. Pregnant. Facing the future alone.

She nodded, letting the tears fall fat and unceremoniously down her cheeks, along and off her chin, darkening the light blue of her linen blouse. They were coming so thick and fast she didn't bother wiping them away.

"I thought I was doing the right thing. If I'd stayed with you—"

"If you'd stayed with me, *what*?" Jamie challenged. "What would have happened if you'd stayed with me? We would've got married? Perhaps had a child by now? Not be here in this—" He swept an arm out along the vista when his anger collapsed. "Well…this is pretty beautiful. I don't regret *this*."

Beatrice spread her hands across her face and

wiped at the tears, laughing despite herself. "You always could see the best in everything."

"You brought that out in me."

"No." She shook his words away. "I don't deserve that. You were good at that before I met you. It's one of the things that made me fall in love with you."

Jamie gave her a sidelong glance. "And what was it exactly that changed how you felt? Did you see something you didn't like? Or something you liked more in *him*? Even though you weren't 'in love' with him."

He hadn't needed to put up air quotes as he spoke. His voice had said it all. The glint of opportunities lost sparked in his green eyes, which flared to show her time *hadn't* healed the wounds she knew she'd inflicted in the way she'd hoped it might.

"Oh, Jamie." Her voice was barely a whisper, and her heart was doing its very best to leap out of her throat.

He could have said a lot of things. Accused her of leaving for the money. For the opulent palazzos she would have lived in. The parties, the traveling, the haute couture she would have been pictured wearing in all the glossy magazines, at all the parties where people cared about those sorts of things. Palaces and pistes. Beaches and ballrooms. The list went on and on, but none of those would have been the answer.

"Why did you do it?" he asked again, his voice hoarse with emotion.

"A little girl trying to please her mother, I suppose," Bea whispered, her voice breaking as she spoke.

She didn't suppose. She knew it. She'd hashed and rehashed it on an endless loop these past few weeks. And the answers she had come up with were sobering. It wasn't entirely her mother's fault. Her family's fault. Even tradition wasn't to blame.

At the end of the day, all the blame lay solidly at her own feet. *She* was the one who had left the man she loved. Put on that white dress. All that ridiculous lace!

The waste.

The heartache.

Heartache she couldn't admit to because, as Jamie had so bluntly put it, their relationship was "water under the bridge." Even if all she wanted to do right now was drop to her knees and beg his forgiveness. Plead with him to believe that she'd never stopped loving him. That she would do anything to make things right again. But it was impossible.

When her ex-fiancé had made it more than clear that she'd be raising her child on her own she had vowed never to enter into a relationship again. Too painful. Too many pitfalls.

And now that the one man she would have made an exception for was in front of her it was like stabbing a dagger into her own heart. But her choice was made. She had to continue alone. Live with the pain. With what she'd done.

There was no way in the world she could ask Jamie to love her child. Raise it. Love it as his own. Not after what she'd done.

She cleared her throat and forced herself to look him straight in the eye. "I guess you could say I fell in line. Our families—the di Jesolos and the Rodolfos—have known each other forever. Generations. It's what our people *do*."

She sought Jamie's eyes for some sort of understanding. Anything to make her feel the tiniest bit better… Nothing. Just a blank expression as if she'd been listing cement prices. His lack of response was chilling.

When he finally spoke his voice bore the toneless disappointment of a judge on the brink of laying down a guilty verdict.

"Do you *really* believe this was entirely your family's doing? That you didn't play *any* role in it?"

Bea's hands flew to cover her chest, as if protecting her heart from his words.

"Well, not entirely, no—but surely you can understand how—"

"No. I can't." He held up his hand, putting an end to her appeal. "Maybe it's culture. Maybe it's class. But *my* family has done nothing but make sacrifices to ensure my life was better."

"And is that your guilt for their sacrifices talking? Or righteous indignation because I made my own sacrifice at the di Jesolo altar? A sacrifice for the greater good of *my* family!"

Bea hated herself for the cruel words. Jamie was the last person she should be lashing out at. The last person whose forgiveness she should expect.

She'd been a fool to think he might be the one

to go to for compassion. For one of those unchecked, bear hugs he used to give. The hugs that had assured her everything would be all right.

She steeled herself and looked him in the eye again. Nothing. The shutters had dropped.

This summer was going to be a test.

Penance for the mistakes she'd made along the way.

And, in the end, perhaps proof that she'd be able to put up with anything once her baby was born.

If she could survive the arctic gaze shredding her nerves right now she could survive anything. Raise a baby on her own. Teach him or her right from wrong…ensure they lived the life they wanted to live.

Steeling herself against that remote gaze of his, she turned to Jamie, matching his tone with a level of cool that took her by surprise. "Like you said, Jamie. People change."

Beatrice might as well have reached in and ripped his heart straight out of his chest.

Of *course* he'd bloody well changed!

Jamie set off with determined, long-legged strides after Beatrice, who had marched away, with quick, tight steps to start and then, when she hit the end of the promenade, stretched her legs into a run.

What did she expect? She'd *left* him. Yanked the world out from under his feet. Smashed his heart into bits. He'd been utterly dumbfounded when she'd left, had made it through each and every day since then through sheer force of will.

Eyes glued on that platinum blond head of hers, he pushed himself harder, even though he didn't have a clue what he was going to say when he reached her.

Tell her to leave.

Beg her to stay.

Either way, this *wasn't* how they were going to leave things. With her storming off in a huff because he wasn't rolling over and placating her ego. She'd left him once and he'd be damned if he was going to see the back of her again unless it was by mutual agreement.

Furious that he'd let things degenerate between them so quickly, Jamie reached out and grabbed Beatrice's elbow. The move threw her off balance, so he quickly stabilized her with both hands, holding her square in his arms. The two of them were breathing heavily, eyeing each other in anticipation of who would make the first move.

Before he could think better of it he cupped her chin in his hand, tipped her lips toward his and kissed her as if his life depended upon it. At this very moment, tasting her, feeling her respond to him as passionately as she was, sure as hell felt as if it did.

As suddenly as the moment began it was over. He wasn't sure who had pulled back first or if they'd simply needed to come up for air. Either way, he was sure of one thing. Beatrice was right. She hadn't left him because she didn't love him. It was still there. The spark. The fire.

Knowing that made the whole scenario worse.

If he couldn't count on her to stick with him through thick and thin there was little point in asking her to try again. No way would he be able to pick up the pieces a second time.

He stepped back and away from her, his hands scrubbing at the back of his head as if his fingers could reach in and reestablish the order he'd only just put into place.

"I shouldn't have done that."

Beatrice didn't say anything, pressing her fingers into her kiss-stung lips. Her eyes were wide, red rimmed with the tears she'd already shed.

"Let me walk you home." He stuffed his hands into his pockets to stop himself from pulling her into a hug, stroking her hair, whispering to her all those things a man told a woman when he knew she was hurting and wanted it to stop.

"Don't worry." She shook her head, took a quick scan of the piazza as if to regain her bearings. "It's been a long day. I'd like to walk home alone, if you don't mind."

It came out as almost a question. Just the merest hint of her genuinely caring if he *did*, in fact, mind.

"Do you want to make this work?" he asked instead. "The working-together thing?" he continued when she looked up at him, eyes as wide as saucers.

"I do." She nodded, her voice more solid than he'd heard it all day.

"Well, then… Looks like we'd both better get some rest. Tomorrow's going to be a long day."

And without a second glance he turned and walked away.

CHAPTER FOUR

"AM I ALLOWED to take showers with this on?"

Bea smiled. Since when were thirteen-year-old boys worried about *showers*?

"He means *go swimming*," his mother interjected, rubbing a hand through her son's sandy blond hair. "*Il est mon fils*. He's my son and he's like me," she translated, though they had been speaking French for most of the time Bea had been circling the colored fiberglass wrap onto the boy's arm. "He's addicted to the lake. My little minnow."

Guillaume squirmed and muttered something about not being so little anymore. Probably a teenage growth spurt and a lack of awareness of his new gangly limbs were the reason behind his fall. It also explained why rock climbing might not have been the best choice of activity.

Bea finished off the task with a smile, smoothing the last bit of blue wrap onto his arm. "Good thing you were wearing a helmet."

They all turned to look at the multicolored helmet, which had received an almighty dent in the boy's fall.

"You know, your cast is made out of the same thing as your helmet. It should keep your arm safe until you heal, but unfortunately it's not one hundred percent waterproof. I've put a waterproof liner in there, and I can get you a waterproof sheath—but it's not a perfect guarantee it will stay dry."

"I can pretty much guarantee, now that you've said that, Guillaume is going to be in that lake straightaway."

Bea laughed. "If you can bear it, hold off until tomorrow. You want it to dry properly and make sure everything's set. After that—" she looked at the mother "—the main goal is to make sure his skin stays clear of rashes or any other irritation. If you have a hair dryer, use the cool setting to dry inside the cast if it does get wet."

The mother and son looked at each other and laughed. "Marie is *never* going to let me borrow her hair dryer!"

"Perhaps if you asked nicely, instead of teasing her all the time." His mother gave him an elbow in the ribs.

"Older sister?"

Mother and son nodded as one.

Bea busied herself with tidying away the packaging from the wrap, wondering if she and *her* child would share moments like that. The relaxed camaraderie. So different from what she'd grown up with.

Clearing her throat, she banished the thought. She had to get through the pregnancy first.

"A vacuum cleaner works just as well."

"Ah!" Guillaume's mother laughed again. "If only my son weren't allergic to cleaning! I doubt he even knows there's a vacuum cleaner in our cottage."

Guillaume pretended not to hear, tapping away at his cast, examining the multiple colors his fingers were already turning in the wake of the break.

"I can't wait to show Marie my X-rays. She'll have to take back everything she said about me crying for nothing."

Bea pushed back on her wheeled stool as the

boy's mother put her arm around her son's shoulder and pulled him in for a gentle hug. "It's all right to cry, *mon amour.* Strong men *should* show their feelings."

He wriggled in embarrassment, but didn't pull away.

Bea looked away again, fastidiously training her eyes on the paperwork.

It seemed every single thing in the universe was a little lesson, guiding her toward impending motherhood.

Moments like these would soon be in the pipeline for her. Trips to A&E. The frantic worry that her son or daughter would be all right. The relief, flooding through her when she was assured her child would be just fine. The love shining through it all.

"Let's get back to your *papa*, shall we, Guillaume? Show him your latest achievement."

The smile stayed on Bea's lips as she handed over the release papers, but inside, her heart had cinched tight.

That was the missing ingredient in her life. A father for her tiny little child.

Her fingers instinctively moved up to her lips,

reliving that kiss. Even though it was a week ago now, in those few precious moments she'd thought maybe…just *maybe*…

"Is there anything else, Dr. Jesolo?"

Bea shook her head, unwilling to allow the wobble she knew she'd hear in her voice if she spoke.

Pointing the pair in the right direction, she curled her fingers around the cubicle curtain and tugged it shut, needing just a few seconds to compose herself. Another rush of tears. Another case of embedding the emotions of each of her patients straight into the fabric of her soul, of not being entirely able to retain her professional distance.

Hormones, no doubt.

All of a sudden Beatrice's eyes snapped wide-open. Was that really what she'd thought it was? Just the tiniest of flutters and yet…

Her hands slid instinctively across her belly… *Oh! Yes.* There it was again. Like having a butterfly inside her, but so much better.

Years of medical training told her it *couldn't* be what she thought it was. That precious little life letting her know that he or she was in there.

It was far too soon to feel anything. There were all sorts of other possibilities. Medical explanations.

A need to pee. *Again.* An increase of blood flow to her womb, drawing her attention to the area. The fact that the low waistline of her skirt was becoming the tiniest bit more snug, despite weeks of morning sickness.

Either way, she believed the sensation *was* her tiny, precious baby letting her know he or she was alive in there.

"Can I get a hand here?"

Bea pulled her stethoscope around her neck and ran, not even bothering to take a swipe at the tears she didn't seem to be able to control. Happy or sad, they appeared on tap these days. Allergies, she told everyone.

Jamie.

Her focus was so complete as she ran to the triage area she hardly noticed that he had moved in alongside her as two gurneys were wheeled in by paramedics.

"Here." He handed her a disposable surgical gown. "Better put this on. Things might get messy."

"What's happened?" She saw Jamie's double take as she swept away the remnants of emotion before turning her full attention to the patients and the paramedic rattling off their status.

"Two women presenting with second- and third-degree burns."

"Where's my wife?" A man pushed through the swing doors, his eyes frantic with worry.

"She's here with us. Exactly where she needs to be." Jamie's solid voice assured the man.

"I *told* her not to use that kerosene stove. It didn't look safe. I *told* her it didn't look safe!"

Bea threw her attention to the woman on the gurney closest to her as she heard Jamie continuing to placate the man, convincing him to go back to the waiting room to be with his other children.

"Why are her clothes all wet?" she asked.

"When the stove exploded she jumped into the lake!" the woman's husband shouted over Jamie's shoulder.

"Second- and third-degree burns." Dr. Brandisi appeared on the other side of the gurney, his gloved hands at the back of his neck as he tied on his disposable gown. It was critical the wounds were kept as hygienic as possible. Infection was a burn victim's worst enemy. "We need to start cutting these clothes off."

Bea did her best to soothe the woman, although she was unable to run a hand across her brow as the flames had hit her forehead.

"What's your name, *amore*?"

"My sister!" The woman struggled to push herself up. "Is my sister here?"

"She's blistering. Only remove what isn't anywhere near the burns." Jamie's voice came through loud and clear as he took control of the team. "We need Brandisi and Bates with the sister. Her name's Jessica. Dr. Jesolo?" Jamie's eyes hit Bea's as she tied on a face mask. "This is Monica Tibbs. You're with me."

Bea nodded, not questioning his assignment for an instant. To do so would waste precious time. Just a rough glance told her that somewhere around thirty percent of Monica's body had taken a hit from the explosion. The damage was significant.

The calm with which Jamie approached the chaotic situation infused everyone with much needed focus. Collectively, they went to work.

Instructions, low and urgent, flew from doctor to doctor, nurse to nurse.

Bea didn't have time or any need to worry about the fact that Jamie was now by her side, carefully cutting along the length of the woman's trouser leg. Pieces of cloth stuck to her skin. It was hard to look at. Essential to treat.

"Jessica's lost consciousness." Dr. Brandisi's voice rose above the rest. "Can we get a check on her stats, please?"

"Where's the oxygen? We need to get some oxygen."

"It's impossible to attach the monitor tabs."

"Use your fingers. The woman's still got pulse points."

The tension in the room ratcheted up another notch. After a moment of taut silence and furious concentration a nurse rattled off some numbers. The voices rose around Jessica's bed, then dropped just as suddenly.

"What's going on?" Monica whispered.

"Can we get an intubation kit?" Dr. Brandisi asked.

"Anyone clear on the ambient temperature? We don't want to add hypo to the symptoms."

Jamie threw the question over his shoulder to the stand-by staff awaiting orders.

"They're doing everything they can for your sister," Beatrice told Monica, taking as much of the her top off as she was able to, steering clear of the burns. Thank goodness it was cotton. A synthetic top would have melted instantly. "Hypothermia can be a problem if the room's too cool and there's a large burn surface."

"I never should've suggested making pancakes! It was ridiculous!"

"There's soot in Jessica's airway."

"Better that than losing oxygen."

"She's not breathing?" Monica rasped, lifting the oxygen mask from her mouth, her throat losing its battle for moisture.

Bea looked across to Jamie. He nodded. She knew that nod. *Go ahead and be honest*, it said. *But do it with care.*

Bea ran her fingers as gently as she could against the unburnt skin of the woman's cheek. "This team of doctors are exactly who she needs to be with right now. Let us focus on you."

"Give me a moment." Dr. Brandisi silenced his team as they prepared to intubate Jessica.

"All right—we're in. Let's get her into surgery, people."

As one, the team flicked switches, unlocked wheels, tugged rolling IV stands close and moved toward the swinging doors that led to the small surgical ward.

"Is my sister going to be all right?" Monica tried to sit up again, screaming when her exposed arm brushed against the side of the gurney. "Cut it off!" she pleaded, her one good hand clutching at Bea's surgical gown. "Please—cut it off if you have to, but make the pain stop!"

"We're doing everything we can. As soon as your IV is in, the pain will begin to ease." Bea turned to the nurse hanging up the bag of electrolyte fluid. "How much lidocaine do you have in there?"

The nurse told her she'd used the standard calculation.

"Ten milliliters to a five hundred milligram bag?"

The nurse nodded.

"There isn't any potassium in the bag, right?"

"No. We've heard about the risks. Even up here in the hinterlands."

Bea's eyes flicked to Jamie's at the comment. She hadn't been questioning the nurse—just making sure all the bases were covered.

She returned her attention to Monica. This wasn't the time to bicker about whose pool of knowledge was bigger, even if her specialty *had* been trauma. Malnutrition and respiratory infections had been her bread and butter at the charity clinic in Venice, but today she was going to have to draw on every ounce of experience she'd had at Northern General. And rely on Jamie. This was *his* turf. His call to make.

"I know it's difficult, Monica, but if you could lie back it will help with the pain." Her eyes flicked to Jamie. Which way would he want to go with this?

"Have you done the fluids calculation for the first twenty-four?" Jamie asked. He had removed all the clothing he could from Monica's side and begun checking her circumferential burns.

"Four mils multiplied by the patient's body weight by TBSA?" She winced. She hadn't meant it to sound like a question.

"You've got it." He didn't sound surprised. "Make sure fifty percent of that is fed through in the first eight hours, the rest infused over the last sixteen. Are you all right to oversee this?"

"Sure." Bea turned to the nurse and asked for extra bags of the electrolyte solutions essential for rehydrating the patient, along with giving her a request to monitor the urine output.

"I'm swabbing for microbiological contamination."

Jamie looked to Bea. Again, as if reading his mind, she knew what he was saying. *Brace your patient.* It would hurt, but Monica had been in a lake. They had to know what germs they'd be fighting.

After talking Monica through the pain of the swabs, Bea returned her attention to Jamie. If he was needed for other cases she should show she was on top of this. Or was he babysitting her? Making sure nothing else had changed about the woman he'd thought he'd known inside and out?

Either way, it just showed he was a good doctor. It wasn't anything to get bristly about.

"Warm water wash before dressing, and then what would you like?"

"We'll need a CBC and ABG, a check on urea and electrolytes." Jamie turned to the nurse.

"Would you please get Monica's blood glucose levels, B-HCG and an albumin test?"

"What *is* all that? Am I going to live?" Monica's hoarse voice croaked up through the list of instructions.

"We're doing our best to get you through this," Bea replied.

She would have loved to say yes. Make assurances. But burns this big opened a patient up to multiple complications. The tests Jamie had ordered were only the beginning of weeks, if not months of treatment. The poor woman would no doubt need extensive time with multiple therapists as her body was healed from its devastating injuries. Luckily, it seemed most of hers were second-degree burns—unlike her sister, who seemed to have taken the bulk of the fireball's heat.

"We need to get some saline into her. And some blood. Her heart's going to need all the help it can get." Jamie nodded at Beatrice to get the IV. "Anyone ascertained a blood type?"

"O positive," answered a dark-haired nurse, Giulietta. "And her husband said she doesn't have any allergies. Do you want me to organize a transfusion?"

"Not just yet. Let's see how she goes with the rehydration solutions and lidocaine first. Dr. Jesolo, have you established the TBSA yet?"

Beatrice pulled a sterile needle from its packaging and prepared to inject antibiotics into the fresh IV bag. "To me it looks like thirty percent. Maybe a little bit more."

He nodded. "Good." His eyes flicked to Giulietta. "Can we get a call in to the burns unit in Pisa? These two are going to need to be transferred as soon as they're stabilized."

"They're from the UK. Is it worth putting a call into a hospital there? A medevac?"

He shook his head. The hospitals in the UK were terrific, but time was a factor. "Let's get her stabilized and en route to Pisa for the time being. We'll call in a translator if necessary."

"Yes, Dr. Coutts."

Another nurse filled her spot as quickly as Giulietta left.

"I'm just going to check on Jessica—are you all right on your own?" He knew what the answer would be, but wanted to triple-check with

Beatrice. There was something a bit fragile about her today. Something in direct contrast to the slight bloom he'd thought he could see in her cheeks when she'd come in this morning. He'd been a fool to cross the line as he had with that blasted kiss, but it was too late to wish it back now.

"We're going to be just fine here. Aren't we, Monica?"

Jamie watched as Beatrice bent close to her patient's lips, listening intently as a message was relayed.

When she looked up at him, there were tears in her eyes. "Could you let Jessica know that her sister loves her?"

"Of course." Jamie nodded somberly as he met Beatrice's gaze.

They both knew how severe these two cases were. How, even if their patients survived the blast, their lives would be changed forever.

"Straightaway."

From the moment he entered the operating theater he sensed something was wrong.

The instant he heard the words *hypovolemic shock*, his mind went into overdrive.

Jessica's extensive burns meant her body couldn't retain fluids—crucially, blood.

Dr. Brandisi gave Jamie a curt nod when he joined the table, tying on a fresh gown as he did so. "We can't get enough blood into her. Or saline fluids. Her heart's beginning to fail."

"Raise the feet, please." It was a last-ditch attempt to try to increase her circulation, but a quick glimpse at her heart rate and pulse were sure signs that there was little hope. The atmosphere in the room intensified.

"I don't suppose there are any peristaltic pumps hidden in a cupboard somewhere," he said to no one in particular. He knew as well as everyone else that there weren't, and rehydrating the patient was critical. Despite the fact they were a midsize clinic, they simply weren't equipped to deal with an injury of this nature.

"Negative," Teo replied needlessly, his expression grim. "The chopper is on its way. Potassium levels are too high. Can we try to get more fluids in her?"

"She's going into cardiac arrest."

"Kidneys are failing."

"Temperature's falling. Let's not add hypothermia to the list, people!"

Jamie scanned the woman's chest. The burns were too deep to consider using the standard defibrillation equipment. They could try for open-heart surgery, but they simply didn't have the means of getting enough blood into her body to warrant any success.

As the team worked with a feverish intensity, Jamie did what he had promised. Jessica's chances were fading with each passing moment, and he sure as hell wasn't going to let her die without hearing her sister's words. He knelt low beside her, gently holding each side of her head as he did so, and passed on the message of love.

All too quickly the team had exhausted every means of keeping Jessica alive.

"Do you want to call it?" Teo stood back from the operating table, angrily pulling his gloves off and throwing them in the bin. No one liked to lose a patient. No one liked to make the call.

Jamie glanced up at the digital clock as he pulled off his own gloves. "Time of death—"

"The helicopter's here. Are you ready?"

Beatrice burst through the doors of the operating theater holding a mask in front of her face, her eyes darting around the room until they landed on Jamie.

"Time of death," he repeated, with more feeling than he'd anticipated, "nine-oh-seven."

Beatrice dropped the mask, a flash of dismay darkening her features before she quickly composed herself. She gave Jamie a quick nod. "I'll let the staff know. I might hold off on telling the sister until her transfer is complete."

"As you see fit," Jamie agreed.

It was always a delicate balance. Family desperate for information. Taking it hard. Losing the will to survive. Monica's burns were severe, and she would need every ounce of fight she had left in her.

He nodded his thanks to the support team and went out through the back of the clinic for just a moment to recover. Regroup.

Behind the clinic was a small courtyard, paved with big slabs of mountain granite. One of the nurses kept the flower boxes bright with fresh blooms. They were a cheery, lively contrast to the hollow sensation that never failed to hit him whenever their efforts failed.

He heard the helicopter rotors begin their slow *phwamp, phwamp*, building up speed and ultimately taking off, banking to the south to head for the burns unit in Pisa.

His thoughts were with Monica's husband, still in Casualty with his children, where the nurses and doctors were tending to their minor injuries. His holiday up in the mountains turned into a living nightmare.

Jamie wouldn't have wished what they were going through on anyone.

It was a vivid reminder that no matter how difficult he'd found it to see Beatrice these past few days, she was *alive*. While they were obviously still stinging from their breakup, neither of them was going to have to deal with the physical traumas Monica would for the rest of her life.

The poor woman would have to focus with all the power of her being on the silver linings. Her children had escaped injury for the most part. Her husband was fine, dedicated to his family and their welfare. Monica would bear the scars of this day forever, but in her heart she would be eternally grateful for pulling through.

He looked up into the bright blue sky, dappled with a smattering of big cotton-ball clouds. He picked one and stared, squinting against the brightness of the morning sun as it rose at the far end of the lake.

So Beatrice had left him to do right by her family. She had never been a woman to take a decision lightly, so there must have been something deep within her, compelling her to choose to fall in and play the good daughter. *His* family had made sacrifices for him. Life-changing sacrifices so that he wouldn't have to. What if he had been put in a similar situation?

He closed his eyes and let the sun beat down on his face.

His family wouldn't have *had* a similar situation, but he knew that if push had come to shove he'd have laid his life on the line for any single member. It would be two-faced of him not to expect Beatrice to do the same.

At the time her decision had hurt as badly as if she'd stabbed him and left him for dead. But she'd never said she didn't love him. Never said she didn't care. And when he'd kissed her… The sensation had kept him up near enough half the night. He knew what he had felt—and it was about as close to love as he dared let himself believe.

He opened his eyes, surprised to feel a soft smile playing on his lips. Tough start to the day. But it had given him some much needed perspective. A way to get through the summer with his heart intact.

It was at moments like these that Bea felt overwhelmed by the beauty of the human spirit.

The day had been a long one and having heard at long last that Monica had arrived at the specialist burns unit and was receiving the best treatment she could get, Bea had felt the tightness in her chest loosen a bit. When the doctor changing shifts with her had mentioned the community's response to the accident she'd taken a walk down to the lake, and the sight that greeted her now set her heart aglow.

The lake was sparkling so brightly it looked as if it were inhabited by thousands of tiny stars, and out of respect for the family who had suffered such a heavy loss today holidaymakers and locals had joined forces, piling huge bouquets of flowers on the boat launch where the accident had taken place. As the sun set one by one people were releasing floating candles onto the lake. Hundreds of people had turned up. The overall effect—shimmery, magical, otherworldly—was healing.

"Quite a turnout."

A spray of goose bumps rippled up her arms. No need to turn around to guess the man behind the voice. But before she could think better of it Bea did turn, her body registering Jamie's presence and her brain still spinning to catch up, as if her skin remembered what it was like to be touched by him without a prompt.

Little wonder. When she'd agreed to the arranged marriage she had forced herself to preserve her time in England in a little memory bubble and hide it as far away as she could. How else would she have survived?

And now that she was pregnant... *Oh, Dio!* It was as if the bubble had been sliced open and her dream man had been put in front of her just in case she hadn't already known what she'd given up.

She was going to have to find a way to be stronger than this, better than this, when her child was born. There was no way her baby was going to suffer for her own madness-fueled mistake. Because it did boil down to just one. Leaving Jamie.

"Really good work today." Jamie tucked his chin down so that his eyes were on a level with hers. A move he'd once used to great effect to tug a smile out of her after a rough shift.

She swallowed before she answered, knowing those ever-ready tears would come if she spoke straightaway. "You, too." She went for a casual, buddy tone. "I'd almost forgotten how well we work together."

"I hadn't." He pushed up to his full height, eyes looking out upon the lake. "Look, do you see there, where the moonlight meets up with the candles? It's as if they're drawn to one another."

Unable to respond, she murmured an acknowledgment and looked back out at the lake.

Drawn to each other...

Just like the pair of them. She'd used to think their combined energies made them a force to be reckoned with. Now, with the situation she'd found herself in—correction, *put* herself in—she was a moth drawn to the flame. Falling in love with Jamie again would be all consuming. Something she wouldn't be able to come back from.

In a few months' time she would need to give all her energy to her child. Figure out how to pay the bills. Work. Breastfeed. Love. Laugh. Cry. All of it with one sole focus. Her newborn child.

So right here and now, opening up the heart she knew was near to bursting with love for the man she'd left behind wasn't an option.

They stood for a few moments in silence, gazing out at the lake. The area was crowded, and there wasn't much room. Someone trying to get a lakeside view caught Bea off balance, and despite her best attempts not to reach out to regain her balance her hands widened and found purchase on Jamie's chest. His arms automatically cinched around her back, creating a protective barrier by pulling her in close to his chest.

Bea was hit by a raft of sensations.

The scents she would have been unable to describe a fortnight earlier came to her now as clear as day. Cotton. Cedar. Spice and citrus.

The feel of the firm wall of chest her fingers hadn't been able to resist pressing into.

The memory of being able to tuck her head in that secure nook between his shoulder and chin, her forehead once getting a tickle when he'd experimented with growing a beard.

Despite herself, she laughed.

"What's so funny?" Jamie asked, pulling back to examine her.

"Do you remember when you wanted to grow a beard? It was wintertime, wasn't it?"

"Winter into spring," he answered, the memory lighting up his own eyes as he spoke. "That's why I ended up shaving it off." He scrubbed a hand along his bare chin. "That thing itched something crazy once the weather started warming up. What made you remember that?"

"Just popped into my head." A white lie. What else was she going to say? *Being this close to you made me want to nestle into your chest and relive some of the most perfect moments of my life?* Hardly.

"Memories are funny things." Jamie loosened his hold on her and then dropped his hands to his sides. "I've been having quite a few myself today."

Bea's forehead lifted, though it wasn't in surprise. How *could* he be immune to the fevered trips down memory lane she'd been tearing along from the moment she'd seen him again?

"Shall we?" Jamie tipped his head toward the square, where the crowd was less thick.

She shook her head. "I should probably be getting back to my apartment. I'm an early-to-bed sort of woman these days."

"No more double alarms?"

They both laughed at the memory and she shook her head. No. That had all changed.

"I'm up with the lark these days," she said, grateful for the reprieve from looking into Jamie's beautiful green eyes when he turned to forge a path through the crowd for the pair of them.

When they'd been together she'd slept like a log. So deeply she would turn off her alarm without even remembering having batted around in the dark to stop its beeping.

That had all changed when she'd returned to Italy. She'd blamed it on the one-hour time difference knowing full well it was nerves. A permanent feeling of foreboding, as if she *knew* marrying Marco would never bring her the joy loving Jamie had.

She stared at his back as he worked his way steadily, gently through the crowd. If she'd been with him she would never have…

Ugh. Sigh.

She would never have done a lot of things.

Like agreeing to have an IVF "honeymoon baby." Marco had pushed her into it so that no one would know he was infertile. Completely incapable of providing the Rodolfos with the heir they craved.

Not that she'd ever jumped into bed with him to see if the doctors had been wrong.

And not that he'd protested.

Having this mystery baby had never been a question for her. It was hardly the child's fault she'd agreed to marry someone whose pedigree rendered him more playboy than prince.

The only relief she felt now was that the baby wasn't his. The way things stood, the child growing inside her belly was one hundred percent hers and hers alone.

"Time for a drink?" Jamie asked over his

shoulder, as if sensing the discord furrowing her brow.

She shook her head. "I shouldn't really."

"I won't bite. Scout's honor." He turned, crossed his heart, then held up his fingers looking every bit the Boy Scout she knew he'd once been.

"Are you still in touch with your old den leader?"

"Dr. Finbar?" He shook his head. "Not for a while." His gaze shifted up and to the right as he made a calculation. "Must be a year or so before I left since I saw him. I should've gone to see him before I up and went, but—" his gaze returned solidly to hers "—I wasn't at my best."

"I'm so sorry, Jamie. If I could have done anything—"

"No." He cut her off. "It wasn't you—it was a patient. Why I left."

Something in his tone told her that wasn't entirely true, but Jamie was allowed his privacy. His pride. He'd been the one left behind to pick up the pieces. To explain to everyone why she'd left after they'd seemed so perfectly happy with each other.

Being humiliated in front of the enormous

crowd at her wedding had served her right. She wouldn't have been the slightest bit surprised to have learned Jamie had raised a glass at the news. A bit of schadenfreude for the embittered suitor.

"How is it you can even face me?" she asked, surprising herself as much as Jamie by the forthright question. "After what I did, I'm surprised you can even speak to me—let alone not hate me."

"Oh, my beauty. *Ma bella Beatrice…*" He pronounced it the Italian way, hitting each vowel and consonant as if he were drinking a fine wine. He stroked the backs of his fingers along the downy soft hairs of her cheek. "I could never hate you. I think I hated myself more than anyone."

A sad smile teased at the corners of his mouth. His lips were fuller than most men's. Sensual. She could have drowned in his kisses, and just the thought of never experiencing one again drew shadows across her heart.

"I can't imagine why you would feel that way. What would make you think so poorly of yourself?"

"Oh…" He clapped his hands together. "About a million reasons. Not putting up a better fight. Not—I don't know—challenging him to a duel? Confronting your parents? Showing them I was every bit as worthy as…"

He paused and swallowed down the name neither of them seemed able to say.

"Water under the bridge." The words rolled off his tongue as if he'd said them a thousand times before in a vain effort to convince himself it was true. "We're both grown-ups. We've moved on. Whatever happened, it happened for a reason, right?"

She shrugged and tried her best to smile, not really coming good on either gesture. The last thing Jamie was to her was water under the bridge. A moment of perfection embedded in her heart was more like it. "Sometimes I'm not so sure."

Jamie shook his head. A clear sign he didn't want her to plead with him. Beg him to try again as she so longed to do.

"We're on different paths now, Beatrice. But it doesn't mean we can't be on friendly terms for the length of your contract. So, what do you say?" He put out his hand in the space between them. "Truce? At the end of the summer you go your way, I go mine?"

A voice inside her head began screaming again and again. *No*, it cried. *No!* But a softer, more insistent voice told her that to do anything other than agree would be unfair. Cruel, even. He'd endured enough. And she didn't deserve him.

She and her baby would find another place, another way to be whole again.

She put her hand out and met his for a solid shake.

"Truce."

CHAPTER FIVE

"IT DEFINITELY LOOKS worse than it is, Hamish." Bea took a step back from her patient and gave him an appraising look. "The stitches should cover the worst of it, but opting out of wearing a helmet while kayaking…? Not a good move."

"But no one else was!" Hamish gave his chest a thump with his fist. "Scotsmen are *hard*!"

"Doesn't make them smart. You could've been a trendsetter. Using what's *inside* your head instead of bashing the outside of it on a boulder!"

She tried to keep the admonishment gentle, but threw him a stern look as she tugged off her gloves and popped them in the bin. He had a pretty deep gash in his forehead, and if it hadn't been for one of his friends pulling him back up into the kayak and keeping a compress on it until they arrived at the clinic he might easily have died.

"You're going to have to keep the dressing dry

and—" she wagged an admonishing finger at him "—you need to let your friends know one of them is going to have to stay with you at all times for the next two days. Concussion watch."

"*Ach, no!* I've still got another few days here!" The young man protested. "I've been saving for *months*!"

"You could very well have a concussion." Bea pressed down on his shoulders when he tried to get up from the exam table and wobbled. "Any dizziness, nausea, headaches…all signs of a concussion."

"It's all right, Doc!" Her patient waved off her concerns and launched himself toward the curtains around the exam room.

"Hold on!" Bea ran the few steps toward him and tried to get under his arm to support him, but he pulled away and brought them both crashing to the ground.

Her instinct was to pull away. Protect her stomach. She knew the baby was still only teensy—tiny—but she'd already messed up her own life. She wasn't prepared to mess up the little innocent soul inside her.

Seconds later she felt a pair of hands pulling her up.

"Are you all right?"

Jamie's rich voice swept along her spine as she lurched into an upright position, far too aware of how close they were to one another. One arm was grazing against his chest. And her breasts. Ooh…that was a sensual trip down memory lane she didn't need to take. Especially with everything in her body on high alert.

Touch.

Sensation.

The pair of lips just millimeters away from her own. The bottom lip fuller than the top. Just perfect for nibbling. A bit of blond stubble around them, highlighting just how soft those lips were to touch in contrast to the tickle of his five-o'clock shadow…

"Beatrice?" She felt Jamie's grip tighten on her forearms. "Your patient is waiting."

Pregnancy brain be damned!

As quickly as she could, Bea wriggled out of Jamie's arms, unsure just how many precious moments she'd lost to daydreaming about his mouth. And kissing it.

Another shot of heat swirled around her belly. *Santo cielo!*

"*Si, Dottore*. I'm fine. *Grazie*." He could play the white knight all he wanted, but she needed to prove to herself she could stand on her own two feet.

"Are you sure you're okay to treat this patient?" He rocked back on his heels, his eyelids dropping to half-mast as if he were suddenly in doubt as to her skills as a physician. Desired effect or not, it slammed her back into the moment. She might be a lot of things, but she was no slouch as a doctor.

"*Si, Dottore*. If you'll excuse me? Hamish and I have to finish our discussion about concussions."

"I think I'll join you."

Her eyes flicked to his, searching them for more meaning than she could glean from his neutral tone.

"In case Mr.—" He leaned over her shoulder to glance at the patient assignment board, giving her another waft of undiluted alpha Jamie. "In case Mr. McGregor, here, decides to take matters into his own hands again."

Beatrice didn't know whether to be relieved or furious. Her lips were dangerously close to tipping into a scowl, but ever the professional, she put on a smile, reminding herself she probably would need an extra hand in case Hamish decided to flee the scene again. Concussions were no laughing matter.

"Now, Mr. McGregor—" Jamie gestured toward the exam table "—what do you say we take another look at you?"

He knew he sounded like an uptight by-the-letter diagnostician, but it had thrown him off his axis when he'd seen Beatrice hurtling through the curtains as if in a full-on rugby tackle.

His every instinct had been to protect her. When he'd lifted her up and she'd pulled away from him as if he were made of kryptonite it had more than stung. It had riled him. Which meant he still cared—and that made the silent war he was waging with himself to treat Beatrice as he would treat anyone else even harder.

He had loved her with every pore in his body. And had spent every waking hour since she'd left trying to forget her.

Unsuccessfully, as was beginning to become wildly apparent.

Moving to Italy hadn't helped. The language, the food, the blasted snowcapped mountains were all reminders of her. He should have accepted the job in the Andes. He still could have had his snowcapped mountains, but also extra servings of beef charred on an enormous open fire and about twelve thousand miles between himself and his memories.

As if you could outrun something branded onto your soul…

"Just hold still for a moment," he heard himself saying, going through the examination by rote even as his mind played catch-up with life's strange twist of events. "I want to take a look at your eyes."

"I've already examined the cranial nerves," Beatrice said.

The exam area was small and she was close. Close enough for him to smell the sweet honey-and-flower scent that seemed to travel in her wake.

"Given that Mr. McGregor has had a *second* fall, I thought I'd just check again."

He felt a huff of air hit his neck. One that said, *Why are you treating me like a plebeian? You helped train me. You, of all the people in the world, should know I'm the best.*

Who knew a little puff of air could contain so much sentiment?

"I'm not going to have to pay for this twice, am I?" Hamish asked, leaning around Jamie as if the only real answer could come from Beatrice. He pulled out the pockets of his shorts to show they were empty.

"No. All part of the service." Jamie leaned in closer to the young man with his medical torch, taking note of Hamish's various pupil responses and all the while pretending not to hear Beatrice's sotto voce grumblings behind him.

Caveman this...

Entitled Englishman that...

To her credit, she was saying it all in Italian, so the Scotsman appeared none the wiser.

Despite the fact that her venom was directed straight at him—like verbal darts in his back—Jamie smiled.

If someone had treated *him* like this, he probably would have responded in the same way.

Boorishly barging in and repeating what was a standard exam was straight out of the Cro-Magnon handbook. But he hadn't liked seeing the look of terror on her face as she hit the floor, curling in on herself as if protecting a small child in her arms. It had frightened him. And though he might have closed his heart to the idea of loving her again, he damn well wasn't going to see her hurt. Not on *his* watch.

"Right, Mr. McGregor! It looks as though Dr. Jesolo has done her best by you. What did you recommend in regard to follow-up?"

He turned to Beatrice, only to receive a full hit of Glaring Doctor. Arms crossed tightly over her chest. Foot tapping impatiently. One eyebrow imperiously arched as if in anticipation of another admonishment. Something told him not to laugh if he didn't want to turn that heated gaze to ice.

Through gritted teeth she began detailing what she'd presumably already run through with her patient. Rest. No kayaking or other contact sports—with or without a helmet—for at least forty-eight hours. A close watch by others on whether he was feeling nauseous, dizzy, light-headed, and some paracetamol—

"But no aspirin," Jamie interjected, suddenly feeling playful. They'd used to do this when they went on rounds together. See who could come up with the most obscure information on a case. Out-fact each other.

"I also made it clear to Mr. McGregor that if he loses consciousness, has any clear fluid leaking from his ears or nose, or feels unusually drowsy while awake, he should return immediately."

"Or has a seizure," Jamie couldn't help adding, knowing it would send that eyebrow of hers arcing just a little bit higher on her forehead.

"Or loses power in any part of his body. An arm or a leg, for example."

"And if he has a headache that worsens, that's a definite cause for concern."

"As is consuming any alcohol, engaging in stressful situations or losing eyesight."

This time he couldn't stop himself from smiling. She'd seen through him now. And was meeting him medical beat for beat.

"Perhaps he should also consider returning

if he has problems speaking. Or understanding other people."

"You two are really freaking me out!" Hamish broke into this verbal one-upmanship. "Am I going to totally *die* or something?"

They turned to him as one and began apologizing. Jamie took the moment to recuse himself from any further involvement in the case, faking a pained look at the same time. "I've got to dash. Lovely to see Dr. Jesolo has given such thorough treatment. All the best for the rest of your holiday. Toodle-pip for now!"

He took two long-legged strides, yanked the curtain open and closed it behind him and then looked up to the invisible heavens.

Toodle-pip?

His family would have had a right old laugh at the antiquated expression. One usually used by Britain's upper crust—not a working-class family like his.

He gave his head a shake.

Beatrice.

She was the only one who could put him in a tailspin like this. Truce or no—he was going to have to continue to watch his back if he wanted to be in one piece by the end of the summer.

He shook his head again and headed toward the assignment board to find himself a patient.

Toodle-pip...

Teo looked at Beatrice and Jamie as if they'd both morphed into mountain goats.

"What do you mean, you're not coming? *Everyone* on the last shift is heading out to the piazza for the Midsummer Festa. I think the crew inside are even taking it in turns to run out and get a bite to eat before drinks this evening."

He flicked a thumb toward the main square, where it seemed the town's entire population was headed.

"Gotta meet my missus. She's eating for two and I want to make sure I get a look-in."

Jamie didn't miss the sideways glance Bea shot him from the other side of the doorway they were inhabiting.

Was it hearing about "the missus"? Or the news that she was pregnant that had caught Bea out?

"C'mon, guys!" Teo persisted. "What are you waiting for? Grub's up!"

"Would you like to go, Beatrice? Get a taste of mountain living?"

"I've been to quite a few *festas*," she answered noncommittally, giving an indecipherable shake of the head. Then added, "When I was younger."

It wasn't a yes. But it wasn't a no. From the impatience building on Teo's face it was obvious he was taking it personally.

Okay. Bull. Horns. Time to seize them and make a decision.

"All right, I'll go."

Jamie and Beatrice spoke simultaneously, turning to one another in wide-eyed horror, then just as quickly recovering with an about-face to Teo and swiftly pasted on smiles.

Teo shot wary looks from one to the other. "I'm going to head off, but I guess I'll see you both in the square?"

"The piazza—yes." Beatrice nodded, as if she'd been the one to suggest going to the Midsummer Festa in the first place. "I haven't had cherry *crostata* in years. Just the time of year for it."

Her voice might have sounded enthusiastic, but she didn't make even a hint of a move.

Nor did Jamie.

Again Teo's eyes flicked from one to the other. "So..." he drawled in his lazy Australian accent. "Are either of you planning on going to this brilliant festival anytime in the near future? Or are you going to wait until you can sneak in under the cover of darkness?"

Jamie laughed. Too heartily.

His guffaw sounded about as genuine as Beatrice's giggle.

Not one bit.

Trills of genuine laughter sounded on the streets beyond them. Then came the sound of an orchestra tuning up for the musical entertainment. An opera diva giving an initial run at her higher range.

Strangely, the collection of sounds and the general buzz of excitement reminded him of a night when the two of them had scraped together their small incomes and plumped for a getaway in Blackpool.

The classic seaside resort in Britain might not have been to everyone's taste—particularly a princess raised with all the finer things in life within hand's reach—but Beatrice had loved it.

The over-the-top light displays. The dance halls. The bright pink candy floss.

The memory hit a spot he had once thought he would never be able to return to without a wave of acrimony following in its wake.

They might never be lovers again, but he had really meant it when he'd called a truce. Tonight he would simply be putting his theory to the test: bygones should be bygones.

"Right, Dr. Jesolo. Let's not keep poor Dr. Brandisi waiting any longer. He's obviously desperate to join his wife."

"Girlfriend," Teo corrected. "She's not made an honest man of me yet. Although—" he glanced at his watch "—the wedding's got to be by the end of the summer. The baby's due in October, and I want my child to have happily married parents when he's born."

Beside him, Jamie felt Bea stiffen. No great surprise when the words *happily* and *married* were bandied about, he supposed. Proof that money couldn't buy you happiness. Teo obviously had bundles of the latter, but not much money.

An idea popped into his head.

"How about at *Ferragosto*?"

"Aw, *mate*!" Teo feigned a few boxing jabs at Jamie. "That's *brilliant*. Alessandra will go nuts for that idea. A wedding *and* a festival for the price of one! What's not to love?"

Beatrice abruptly turned away. Wedding talk was probably not high on her agenda. A protective urge to steer the conversation in another direction took hold of him.

"Right!" Jamie clapped his hands, then rubbed them together. "Everyone's at their stations and ready for the next shift. I'm with Teo. Let's get a move on."

Jamie turned to Beatrice, his arm crooked, and a genuine smile began to form on his lips as she tentatively tucked her fingers around his elbow. He gave the tips of her fingers a pat. More akin to one a grandfather might give a granddaughter than a slighted ex-lover to a woman, but they were meant to be friends. And friends didn't caress, stroke or give one another unexpected passionate kisses that reawakened every part of the masculinity he hadn't tapped into in heaven knew how long…

"To the square?"

Beatrice nodded, her cheeks streaked with just a hint of a blush.

A hint of pride took hold in his chest. Though he knew it was best to keep things neutral, he couldn't help but enjoy having made an impact. Knowing he could still bring a touch of pink to those high, aristocratic cheekbones of hers.

"You're looking pretty as a picture tonight, Beatrice."

He meant it, too. Her short-cut hair accentuated the clean line of her jaw, and her dark brown eyes, always inquisitive, absorbed the flower displays already on show at the periphery of the square they were fast approaching. Her tongue darted out to lick her lips when they passed a *pasticceria*, its windows bursting with delectable pastries.

He didn't realize he was humming until Beatrice pulled back a little, her fingers still linked into the crook of his arm, and gave him a sidelong look.

He hadn't hummed since…

He knew exactly how long it had been.

"I'm still the same old me," Jamie said, when her expression remained bemused.

"Hmm…" Her lips tightened, then pushed into a moue before doing the little wiggly thing he'd used to be so familiar with. The telltale sign that she wasn't entirely sure of something.

"C'mon, Beatrice." He lowered his voice so Teo, who was talking away on his phone, wouldn't hear them. "Let's make the best of a—" He stopped, trying to find the best words.

"A bad situation?" Beatrice filled in the words he'd been about to say.

"An awkward one," Jamie parried.

She wasn't going to get away with making this harder than it already was. He'd endured more than enough angst on his own. Reliving those dark, lonely hours he'd fought and survived in front of her…? Not a chance in hell.

"Well—" she gave a quick laugh "—that's probably more accurate. But I have to confess I'm still reeling a bit." She changed the tone of her voice to mimic a film star of yesteryear. "Of all the clinics in all of Italy…" She trailed off, her dark eyes darting anywhere but up at his face.

A hit of defensiveness welled up within him.

He had arrived here first. Well, not in Italy, but at the clinic.

"A clinic geared toward tourists was a good fit for me." *All things considered.*

"But an *Italian* clinic? I still haven't quite managed to figure out why they hired you."

"Thanks very much!" He feigned being affronted, knowing it wasn't what she meant. Even so, it felt a bit like she was drawing a line in the sand.

England—his turf. Italy—hers.

Well, too bad. It didn't work that way.

She laughed again, this time pulling her hand out of his arm to hold her hands up in protest. Though her hand hadn't been there long, his arm felt instantly cool at its absence.

"I didn't mean it that way. You know I think you're an amazing doctor."

Their gazes connected and he saw that she meant it. It would have been so easy to attach more meaning to the compliment. More sentiment. But that time had passed.

"I just meant I thought they would hire a fluent Italian speaker for the post."

"They did. Or near enough."

She turned to him, eyes wide with astonishment. “I didn’t know that.”

“There are a lot of things you don’t know about me.”

He swallowed the bitter words that might have followed. Some men might have done their very best to close off every last detail of a lover who’d chosen another path, but he had found it impossible. Their lives had been too interwoven. Beatrice’s love of her home country had become as much a part of him as his Northern English heritage.

What was spring without stuffed zucchini flowers? Or winter without chestnuts? Scents, sights, smells—they had all vividly shifted when Beatrice had swept into his life like a refreshing spring breeze. Turning dull, dark England into a brighter landscape, only to plunge into darkness again when she left.

After a year of trying to block everything out but work, and then losing the young patient he’d grown far too close to, he’d needed that light again. And the closest he’d been able to get to rekindling that light had been to go to Italy.

“For starters,” he began, by way of a gentler

explanation, "you left your copy of *The Silver Spoon* behind."

"I thought you *hated* cooking!"

"Not anymore."

"But when we were together—" She stopped.

He wondered if she'd actually go there. Try to take him on a trip down memory lane neither of them seemed well equipped for. They'd effectively lived together during the second year they'd been together. Not officially—she'd still had her own apartment—but he doubted her roommate had ever seen her there. He couldn't remember a night when they hadn't fallen asleep, woven into each other's arms.

"I guess a lot of things have changed," Beatrice said finally. "Ah, *va bene*! Look at all the people!"

And just as quickly as they'd been held together by the invisible strands of the past, the strings had snapped with a hit of reality.

CHAPTER SIX

BEATRICE KNEW IT was feeble to duck out of the important conversation they should be having, but guiltily welcomed the approaching *festa*.

Exploring the past was too close to asking for a different future. One with Jamie in it. And she knew she couldn't go there. No matter how much it hurt, she'd have to pretend she was happy as could be with their collegial truce. There couldn't be anything more. She would never be able to forgive herself for what she'd done to him. The lies. The betrayal. If even the tiniest part of her thought Jamie could love her again…

She scrunched her eyes tight until she saw stars.

When she opened them again she saw an entirely different world from the quiet cobbled lanes they'd been walking through. Before them swirled a riot of color, music, laughter and scents that all but exploded in front of them when they rounded the corner into the teeming piazza.

"Looks like we've lost Teo to the crowds."

"Hunting down his fiancée, no doubt," Jamie said, scanning the sea of heads.

At six feet two inches, he was able to see across the top of most of the crowd. She'd always loved his height. Taken comfort in the fact that when she'd needed a hug he'd been able to rest his chin on top of her head, holding her close enough for her to hear the beat of his heart.

A shiver went through her—as if she'd just been in his embrace and then stepped away.

"Are you all right?" Jamie was already taking off his light linen jacket. "Here—put this on."

Without waiting for an answer he draped the coat over her shoulders.

How can you be so chivalrous?

The gesture was both cruel and kind. Kind because that was Jamie, through and through. Cruel in its vivid reminder of what she wouldn't have when her baby was born. Someone to look out for her. To care if she was hot or cold. Frightened or tired.

Another tremble juddered through her, despite

the relative warmth of the night, though experience told her the high altitude would set a chill into the air soon enough. She tugged the lapels of his jacket over her shoulders and dipped her head to receive a deep hit of the scents she knew she'd never forget. Ink. Pine. Cotton.

Her shoulders shook against the fabric. The sorrow she'd carried with her all these years was being released in unforgiving waves, and icy tremors reminded her of the day she'd let such a good man go.

"Do you mind if we head over to the fire pits for a minute?"

"Not at all."

Jamie raised his arm as if he was about to drape it over her shoulders, as he would have when they'd been together. Then, his arm half-aloft, eyes blinking himself back to the present, he remembered otherwise and let it drop to his side.

Beatrice was half-tempted to slip her arms into the sleeves of Jamie's jacket and grab hold of his hand. It was how they'd first realized they'd felt the same way for each other. A surreptitious moment of holding hands in a crowd.

It had been a busy night in Jamie's village. It was actually more of a town, but it had a warm, strong sense of community. Unlike tonight, it had been properly cold—wintry, even. She'd been all zipped up in a thick parka, with a wooly hat on her head designed in some silly holiday theme. A Christmas pudding? She couldn't remember, but she knew it had made Jamie's green eyes light up every time he had turned to her.

"What was that thing we went to?" She didn't look up at him, but could tell he'd turned to look at her. "The one where I wore the funny hat?"

He laughed before he answered. A soft faraway laugh, hinting at the genuine warmth they'd shared.

"Bonfire Night. *Remember, remember...*"

"The fifth of November," she finished for him when he left off with a slight lift to his voice.

It came back to her now, in a wash of distinct memories. Much like this evening, people had filled the historic English town—all thick slabs of stone and austere houses lit up by an enormous pyre in the very center of the square. Music had echoed off the walls and the scents of mulled wine and frying doughnuts had permeated the air. Fairy lights had twinkled from just about anything that was stationary—even some members of the brass band.

But more than any of those things Beatrice remembered Jamie insisting she leave the hospital after a forty-eight-hour shift to come out and enjoy the spectacle. They hadn't kissed. They might not even have hugged. She knew her cheeks had flushed regularly when he'd looked at her, and on the rare occasions when their hands had brushed against each other's… it had been heavenly. Like fairy dust sparkles lighting her up from the inside.

"Do you remember when you were almost speared by those two lads wrestling in Viking helmets?"

"How could I forget?" Bea smiled at the memory for, as frightening as it had been, Jamie had scooped her out of the way, lifting her up and swinging her out of reach of the one-pint-too-many brawlers as if she'd been made of air. Heaven knew she'd felt as if she were walking on air for the rest of the night.

Against her better judgment she let her fingers drop from their too-tight hold on the lapels of Jamie's jacket and let her hands swing alongside her as they strolled past the detailed flower displays. Thousands of buds and petals were arranged in intricate designs. Some religious, others nods to the Midsummer Festa's pagan origins. Either way, they were beautiful.

"It was the first time I ever had a sparkler."

Jamie stopped and stared at her, mouth agape in disbelief. "What? At the ripe old age of—what were you then—twenty-five?"

"Twenty-six," she corrected.

"You always did look young for your age." He winked in an obvious bid to let her know he was teasing.

Trust Jamie to retain his sense of humor in the situation. If she'd been in his shoes? *Ugh.* She didn't know if she could have done it. Swiped the slate clean and tried to work together. She could see he really *was* trying, and knowing that made her feel even worse.

There has to be a day when the guilt ends. When I can make my peace with him.

Her eyes shot up to the sky, barely visible for all the light in the piazza, and she swallowed down the prayer, trying to make it a living, breathing part of her.

If she were going to raise her child she would have to find an inner peace.

"First time with a sparkler..." He shook his head again in wonder. "And there was me thinking you couldn't do *anything* new for a princess."

Bea's hopeful mood evaporated in an instant. She shot quick panicked looks around, fearful in case anyone had overheard, forgetting for a moment that nearly everyone within earshot wouldn't have the slightest clue who she was. The world's gossip magazine readers were looking for a brunette long-haired woman, grief stricken after those sensational altar revelations. Not a short-haired platinum blonde snuggling into her boyfriend's linen jacket.

Well, not *boyfriend*... But to an outsider up until about three seconds ago it might have looked that way.

"Too close to the bone with the princess comment?" Jamie asked, his expression unreadable.

No doubt it was a means of protecting his own feelings. Proof she couldn't help but hurt him when all he'd done was make a lighthearted comment.

Get over yourself! Prove to him you're the woman he once thought you were. Not the princess.

She held up two fingers and pinched them together to signify that, yes, unwittingly or not, his comment *had* stung a little bit.

"You know I never thought of myself that way."

She tried to shrug the moment away, but only ended up fighting the sharp sting of tears gathering high in her throat. She quickly turned away, feigning interest in a small stall selling exquisite posies of wildflowers.

"Signor!" She could hear the vendor appealing to Jamie. "Buy your beautiful woman a small bouquet. *Va bene.* It is midsummer. Without flowers in her hand, she is naked!"

Bea chanced a glance at Jamie, relieved to see he that was laughing. Trust an Italian to insist a woman was naked without flowers. Especially when he was walking with his ex-girlfriend and didn't know she was pregnant from an anonymous donor.

He didn't owe her anything. Least of all…

Wait… Was he…?

"*Per favore, solo uno mazzetto.* To bring a smile to her face again."

There he was again. Indefatigable. The sympathetic, generous man she'd fallen in love with.

Just the sound of Jamie's warm caramel voice—the rich, deep-chested tone he'd used to use when he was trying to coax a smile to her face when she'd had a rough day at the hospital—told her he was doing his best to mend fences.

How could she let him know he didn't owe her a thing?

Bea silently smiled her appreciation, watching as he dug a hand into his pocket, rattling around for some change only to come up empty-handed.

He turned to her, and just as she realized *she* must be the one in possession of his loose change he tugged her around via the lapels of his jacket so that she was square onto him. Achingly slowly, he purposefully slid his hands down the lapels, just skidding along the tops of her hypersensitive breasts, pausing when her breath caught, then continuing until each of his hands found purchase on the edge of a pocket. His fingers dipped into the squares of linen, moving assuredly inside them, grazing her hips as he felt for coins.

Everything inside her was alight with anticipation.

When their eyes met, she knew he had felt it, too. The same thing *she* had felt when their hands had shifted and glanced across each other's time and again on that long-ago Bonfire Night. The tension between them had built until it had been virtually unbearable, until at long last Jamie had finally taken charge of the situation and grasped her hand firmly in his.

And from the moment they had touched…

Fireworks.

"I've got a better idea about where to find supper."

Jamie could hardly believe what he was saying. It was the smooth line of an assured lover. A man confident that if he made a move, he'd win the girl.

Was that why he was doing this? Trying to win back his girl?

A harebrained idea, given how it had ended last time. With him throwing himself into work as if it were the only thing keeping him alive. Neglecting his family. His home. Not that he'd ever been one to be house-proud. But what Beatrice didn't know was that the house of their dreams was sitting as empty as the day he'd bought it. If she'd waited just one more day to tell him her news…

There were so many ifs.

Beatrice was looking up at him, thick lashes framing those perfect chocolate-pot-colored eyes of hers, posy held up to her nose, cheeks still flushed with the remains of a blush. Her lips were nestled among the flower petals and every bit as soft. *Perfection.*

A shot of heat seized his chest as the memory of that stolen kiss worked its way back into his blood flow. Beatrice had made him feel more alive than anyone else in the world and when she'd gone—

Was it foolish or wise to hold on to his pride? Resist what came so naturally?

"What's this idea, then?" she asked, twisting back and forth like a schoolgirl behind her fistful of flowers. "Or are you going to keep it a secret?"

Excitement—or maybe it was just the fairy lights—twinkled in her eyes. She'd always loved an adventure. He had no idea what she got up to in her spare time here. Just went home, he imagined. He'd definitely not seen her in the square since the night he'd pulled her into his arms and reminded himself of everything he should have long forgotten.

She'd played with his heart.

And he'd lived to see another day.

What was that saying he'd learnt from one of the friars on the island?

He heard the monk's voice as clearly as he could now hear the diva launching into a beautiful aria by Puccini.

Che per vendetta mai non sanò piaga.

Revenge never healed a wound.

A renewed sense of purpose gripped his heart, then released it, repurposing the sensation into the first shot of pure happiness he'd felt in years. He would have to say goodbye to Beatrice at the end of the summer. That much was sure. But this time he would do it with his pride intact. His heart at rest.

"As we've lost Teo for the evening, we're going to be heading up on the chairlifts." Jamie gave her an appraising look as she gamely weighed up his proposal. "But first I think we'd better stop at one of these stalls. Get you a shawl. It might be a bit chillier where we're headed."

Beatrice's eyebrows rose. "Should I be worried? You're not going to lock me up in a cave or anything, are you?"

"That all depends," he countered, channeling the man he knew was buried somewhere deep in her heart.

"On..." Beatrice's smile was growing bigger. They'd done this dozens, if not scores of times before. Explored. Found new places to show each other. Watched the delight unfold.

"On how much you like cheese!"

Something flickered in her eyes. Indecision? A hint of reserve? That wasn't like her. To hold back.

Just as quickly it was gone.

"As long as there's plenty of hard cheese. It's my favorite these days."

"Not 'the gooier the better'?"

She shook her head and ran a fingertip along one of the flower buds in her posy before dropping it to her side. "No. I'm all about good old hard Italian cheeses these days. I'll leave the gooey ones to the French."

"All right, then." He offered her his arm again. "I see slivers of pecorino and shavings of parmigiana in your future."

He pressed his hand on top of Beatrice's when she tucked it back into the inner crook of his elbow—with greater comfort than earlier in the evening, he noticed.

A shard of warning sounded in his mind.

This is only temporary. This is putting the past to rest. If you can do this without kissing her, you can do anything.

By the time they got to the stall selling locally woven cashmere scarves, Bea was beginning to feel as if she'd stepped back in time.

Jamie was the very embodiment of… Well… *himself.* She knew it seemed ridiculous, but the man she'd fallen in love with was right here beside her, as if nothing had happened, no hearts had been broken… As if their lives had carried on as one.

And it felt so right. *Real*, even.

Would it be tempting fate if she just allowed herself one night of pure happiness?

"Here—what do you think of this one?" Jamie tugged a beautiful evergreen wrap from the midst of one of the piles. In one fluid move he unfurled the downy, soft cashmere and swirled it around her shoulders.

She brushed her cheek against the fabric, reveling in how silky it felt against her skin. There were fine threads of cream and mixed pastel colors woven throughout the scarf, giving it a greater depth…almost as if it were a wildflower meadow in the midst of an evergreen glade, seen from afar.

Jamie lifted a corner of the scarf and tested it along his own cheek. "Does it do the trick?"

A whirl of heat swirled around her as a vivid memory of Jamie lifting her fingers first to his cheek and then to his lips for a light kiss. Something he'd be doing right now if she hadn't bowed to her mother's wishes…

The tiny slice of space between them filled

with warmth—the exchange of body heat melding them from two bodies into one—But there was another body. A tiny little baby she would love with all her heart.

A wash of longing poured through her so powerfully she almost lost her balance. If that baby was Jamie's…

She began to dig inanely through her handbag for her wallet. "It's perfect."

"Trade you for my coat?" Jamie was already handing a couple of notes to the vendor.

"You don't have to do that."

Why *was* he doing this? Each act of selflessness on his part only served to compound the ache of longing she felt for him. How was she ever going to channel the willpower to leave?

"Of course I do," he countered taking his change and helping Bea slip his jacket from her shoulders and rearrange the wrap.

The wrap was beautiful but, ridiculous as it seemed, just those handful of minutes wearing his jacket had felt heaven-sent.

"Jamie, honestly. You don't owe me a thing."

If anything, she owed him… Well, she owed him the truth for one thing, but since his knowing she still loved him would probably only make things worse, keeping her lips sealed was her self-assigned atonement.

"A beautiful woman deserves beautiful things. I never bought you beautiful things before."

"I never wanted *things*," she chided softly. "You know that."

He nodded. "Even so…"

His eyes flicked away, as if something else had caught his attention, but it was more likely for the same reason she found herself unable to hold eye contact with him for more than a few seconds at a time.

Too painful. Too perfect.

Two years ago the most natural thing for her to do would have been to go up on tiptoe. Give him a kiss. Swipe at his nose with her finger and tip his forehead to hers. The time they'd spent just breathing each other in…*otherworldly.*

She tugged at the edges of her sundress, fighting the instinctive urge to give her belly one of the protective strokes she so often found herself doing these days. A harsh reminder that she was still keeping secrets from Jamie.

Holding back this precious information was

almost physically painful. Because Jamie had once been her port of call for all her thoughts. No editing. No filter. The only person in the world she'd been able to be herself with. None of the frippery and trappings that went with being a princess.

Her brother had cornered the royal market for their family. Why hadn't her mother been content just to let her go?

"Look at these tomatoes!"

She smiled, grateful for the change of tack as Jamie steered her toward a table groaning under a mountain of tomatoes bigger than both her fists joined together.

Beautiful deep reds, oranges and yellows. There were even some green tiger-striped fruits, all piled up in a magnificent display of the summer's early harvest.

"The North of Italy is far more generous than the North of England. My mother wouldn't believe her eyes!"

"My mother wouldn't know what a whole tomato looked like!" Bea shot back.

Both of them laughed, then said as one, *"La donna è mobile!"*

Woman—in this case her mother—was a fickle thing to be sure.

Jamie had heard more than enough stories of Beatrice's mother only deigning to recognize food if it was on a plate at a Michelin-starred restaurant. Deconstructed this… Reimagined that… If it wasn't à la mode, it wasn't in her mother's sphere of what existed in the world.

But she'd never been fickle about her choice for Bea's intended. Her daughter would marry a prince. Such lofty heights for her white-coated daughter, more content in one-use-only surgical scrubs than a ball gown.

"And those peaches. They're the size of a house! They'd fill up the fruit bowl nicely."

Jamie pointed toward another vendor handing out slices of golden fruit dripping with summer sweetness. In true Italian style he was peeling them, then giving slice after juicy slice to wide-eyed passers-by.

Though she was tempted, the Italian in her had to insist upon being a purist.

"As you may recall, any *true* Italian would know these are from the South. Sicilian peaches are… Mmm…" A soft breeze carried a waft of perfumed air her way and suddenly she was ravenous. A pregnancy craving? Or just good old-fashioned hunger? She forced herself to regroup. "Their presence here is near enough sacrilege!"

"Like mayonnaise on chips?" Jamie parried, happily accepting a slice of freshly peeled peach from the farmer and making a big show of enjoying the sweet fruit, rubbing his belly to great effect as he swallowed it down.

"Che schifo!" Bea shuddered away the thought of gooey mayonnaise. "*Anyone* who knows how to eat a chip properly knows it's salt and vinegar if eaten with fish—but only by the seaside—or tomato ketchup if eaten with a hamburger."

Jamie smiled as she recited by rote the "training session" he'd given her. Bea had never eaten a chip in her life. She'd been astonished to hear they'd been a menu staple in his house when he was growing up.

"A man needs to keep up his strength when he goes down the mines..."

Jamie's father had been deadly serious when he'd told her that. Right before sending his wife a saucy wink as he picked up a jug and near enough drowned his potatoes in the thick pool of shiny gravy Jamie's mother had magicked up from the small joint of beef she'd prepared.

That had been a heavenly afternoon.

One of only two times she'd met his parents.

Once it had been just in passing…it might have been that Bonfire Night. Near enough every house had emptied into the town square that night. And, of course, when they'd gone over for traditional Sunday lunch.

Not one ounce of shame had crossed Jamie's features when he brought her to the humble two-up two-down brick house in the middle of a seemingly endless swathe of similar homes. Ironic, considering she'd been too mortified even to consider taking him to her parents' palazzo.

One of the most lavish in the whole of Venice, It was her mother's work, of course. Her father would have been content with simpler furnishings. Less gilding. More wood. Less ostentation. More comfort. He often said a happy wife meant a happy life. It had been the spirit with which she thought she'd approach her arranged marriage. A happy husband meant…

Hmm… Maybe that was the problem.

Nothing really rhymed with husband.

James, on the other hand…

Blame. Shame. Tame. Flame.

She bit down on the inside of her cheek. Maybe that wasn't such a good comparison.

"C'mon—over here, you. No wandering off just yet. You're not getting away that easily." Jamie turned to her, a broad smile on his lips, a second slice of peach pinched gently between his thumb and index finger. "Why not try living dangerously?"

When their gazes connected it was as if he'd flicked a switch, blurring everything around them. All Bea was aware of was the light shining in Jamie's forest green eyes. The tempting slice of peach he was holding between them. His lips just beyond. Lips she knew would taste of peach juice and pure male strength…

He was a rock. He'd been *her* rock. And from the moment she'd left him she had felt more adrift in the world than at any other time in her life.

He slipped the slice of fruit between her parted lips, and for just one incredibly sensual moment her tongue and lips connected with his fingertip. The old Bea would have drawn it into her mouth, given it a swirl with her tongue, grasped the rest of his hand in hers so that she could taste the drops of peach juice on each of his fingertips. She would have met his gaze without a blink of shame, her body growing warm with desire as each second passed.

But she had no claim on him now. No right even to think the decadently sexual thoughts, let alone act on them.

As if reading her mind—or perhaps reminding her of where she stood—Jamie turned away, accepted an antiseptic wipe from the peach vendor, swiped his hands clean of the moment and threw it in the bin.

He turned back to her and smiled, as if they'd just been discussing the weather. "And how did little Beatrice become so au fait with the fruits and vegetables of the world?"

"My…my father, of course." She stumbled awkwardly over the words, and most likely failed miserably to cover the ache of longing she felt for him by adding a jaunty elbow in the ribs. "You know that."

"Yes, I do." Jamie nodded, his lower lip jutting out for a moment, her comment having clearly hit an invisible target. "And there are a lot of things I don't know."

In equal parts Bea felt consumed by a wash of guilt and the powerful urge to tell him everything.

About the pregnancy.

About the separate bedrooms she'd insisted upon prior to agreeing to move into her ex-fiancé's palazzo because something in her just hadn't been ready to give herself to him physically.

The relief when her best friend had blown the whistle at the wedding.

The first full breath of air she had drawn after the wedding dress had dropped from her shoulders, then her hips, and plummeted to the floor in a huge flounce of silk and tulle. Part of her had wanted to shred it to pieces. The other half had just wanted to leave. Which was precisely what she'd done.

Only that time it hadn't hurt at all. Not even close to the searing pain she'd felt when she'd left Jamie.

With Marco, she had felt backed into a corner. Trapped by ancestral duty. Or perhaps, more accurately, by the little girl hoping, for once, to win her mother's approval. The more she thought about it, the more astonishing it was that Jamie had been able to rise above it now. Not just treating her civilly, but pretty much acting as if nothing had happened.

No. She gave her head a shake, knowing she hadn't pinned it down right. Jamie was better than ordinary old "civil." He was treating her with respect. Grace. Chivalry.

"All right, there?" Jamie bent down as he spoke.

Another reminder of his thoughtfulness. Her ex-fiancé wouldn't have noticed if she'd fallen silent, talked too much or even started dancing like a chimpanzee.

She nodded, doing her best to focus on Jamie's hand as he pointed out the small passageway across the square. If she turned to him now he'd see tears in her eyes.

"You feeling up to plunging through the crowds?"

"*Si.* Absolutely." Her voice sounded bright. Too bright. But it would have to do.

Being with Jamie… It was like being whole again.

But he was the one thing she would have to learn to live without.

A few minutes of weaving through the crowd later, they turned onto a small road with lighter foot traffic than the square.

"You sure you're still up for this? It may take an hour or two." Jamie turned and gave Beatrice a smile.

Her reaction was a bit delayed. As if her thoughts had been somewhere else entirely.

"Oh…" She tugged her new wrap around her shoulders a bit more snugly. Protectively. "An hour or two of cheese? Hmm… Let me think…"

Her hips swiveled back and forth beneath the light cotton of her dress. It was too easy to picture her long, slender legs beneath the fabric. The gentle curve and jut of her hip bones. His hands swooping along the smooth expanse of her belly before he slid them along the length of her thighs…

A tug of desire eclipsed his pragmatism. The number of times he'd pulled her to him, snuggled her slender hips between his own, fitted her to him as if they'd been made for each other… and then teased her away, holding her at arm's length, reminding her of the long shifts at the hospital they each had in store.

"We have all the time in the world to make love," he'd murmured into her ear, again and again.

Now he knew it hadn't been enough. A lifetime of Beatrice wouldn't have sated his desire for her. And he'd only had those two precious years.

"You know…you're right." He did a quick about-face, no longer able to go through with the charade of being "just friends."

She looked up at him, startled.

"About what?"

"It'll take too long. The chairlift and all. I'm not even certain they'll be open with the Midsummer Festa."

"What?"

"The *enoteca*. I've been up there a few times when I've needed a break from the clinic. A glass of wine… A bit of cheese and bread… It's lovely."

And it was. But going up there with Beatrice the way he was feeling… Chances were he'd tell her how he really felt. And he couldn't let her have access to that part of his heart. Not anymore.

"It was a silly idea in the first place. There's plenty to eat here. And you said yourself you weren't in the mood for gooey cheese. Um… what if we…" He looked past her to the square—busier now than when they'd left it, if such a thing was possible.

"Actually, Jamie…"

He knew that tone. The polite one. The well-mannered Principessa backing out of an awkward situation.

"I'm feeling a bit tired. Perhaps I'll just head off. We can go to the *enoteca* another time. Rain check?"

When he looked back at Beatrice she appeared to him as if through an entirely new prism… fragile. Delicate. Two things he'd never imagined her to be.

Feminine, yes. But for every ounce of grace and beauty she possessed he'd always thought of her as having a solid core of fierce intellect and passion. More than enough to stand on her own two feet.

"I'm happy to walk you back to your apartment. You're not too far from the clinic?"

"*Si*, an apartment in one of the *baita*." She held up her hand in the stop position and took a step away from him. "Don't worry about walking me. There's a little café downstairs. I'll grab something there. I could do with a quiet stroll."

Guilt swept through him. He wanted to pull her to him, wanted to push her away. "I don't mind, honestly."

From the look she shot him it was pretty easy to tell *she* did.

Hell. There wasn't exactly a guidebook on how to deal with the love of your life reappearing just when you thought you'd pulled yourself together.

"Thanks for the wrap." She threw the words over her shoulder, smoothing her hand along the fine cashmere, her feet already picking up speed. "It's really beautiful. *Buonanotte.*"

He said the same words as he spun in the opposite direction, felt the hard lines of a man trying to keep his head above water returning to his face.

It wouldn't be a *good* night. He felt it in his bones. It would be restless. His pillow would bear the brunt of his frustration.

He shifted course, taking a sharp turn into a *calle* that would deposit him at the only place he could burn off this excess energy for the greater good. *Work.*

Sure, it hadn't worked out well at Northern General, but one of the reasons he'd chosen a clinic for tourists was the limited chance of getting attached. People were in, out, referred, transferred, never to be seen again. Only rarely did they see a patient twice. Enough times to start caring? Just about never.

He gave his hands a quick rub, forcing the doctor back into this man he'd not seen for a while. Peach slices? Cashmere wraps? Those were things lovers shared. Not platonic colleagues.

He steered his thoughts away from the glow he'd seen in Beatrice's eyes when he'd slipped the peach between her gently parted lips. There were bound to be people who enjoyed a bit too much high-altitude revelry on a night like tonight. Sprains, dehydration, the occasional fallout from a silly brawl over the last piece of prosciutto… They would keep him busy. The staff at the clinic wouldn't think anything of him showing up to relieve them for an hour or so.

A huge boom sounded not too far-off. He looked up to the sky, his eyes adjusting to the darkness and then the explosion of colored lights.

Instantly he dropped his gaze and sought out Beatrice's pixie cut. She should be seeing this. They should be watching it together. Hands brushing. Shots of heat igniting his every nerve ending as if he was discovering what it meant to be a man for the very first time.

He looked up into the sky one last time then turned back toward the clinic with a shrug.

Fireworks.

They weren't all they were cracked up to be.

CHAPTER SEVEN

BEA KNEW SHE should be at home, but restless sleep was worse than a bit of focused work, right? Just the idea of going back to her lonely apartment, with its plain single bed, and no green-eyed pediatricians lying in wait to pull up the covers and have a good snuggle…

"Are you sure you're happy to cover for me?" Rhianna handed over a stethoscope, not even waiting for an answer.

"You said a couple of hours, right?"

She smiled as Rhianna turned her Irish brogue up another notch and launched into an assurance that, with heaven as her witness, she'd be back before Cinderella had a blessed thing to be worried about.

Bea pursed her lips and gave them a little wriggle. The fairy-tale princess reference wasn't lost on her, but a quick glance to Rhianna, who was busy slicking on a fresh layer of lip gloss and lavishing her lashes with a thick coat of mascara showed she was being silly.

Stop being so sensitive!

Bea sat down on the long wooden bench and undid the straps of her sandals to change them for her sneakers, surprised to see her feet were a tiny bit swollen. Pregnancy symptom? Her mind raced through all the worst-case scenarios swollen feet at this point in a pregnancy might mean, then gave her head a sharp shake.

Probably just too much walking in flat sandals and having all her hopes and dreams plummet to the soles of her feet. Or something like that anyway.

"Ooh!" She put on a cockney accent and repeated something she'd heard a teenager say the other day as she gave her feet a rub. "My dogs are *barking*!"

"Hold on, there." Rhianna ducked her head down so she was level with Beatrice's eyes. Quite the feat now she'd popped on impossibly high cork-heeled sandals. "Is that you backing out already?" She swiftly pulled out her mobile phone and held it at arm's length. "Am I going to have to send a text to the lads and tell them no?"

"The lads?" Beatrice raised her eyebrows. She'd heard of a few summer romances beginning to blossom among the collection of seasonal staff, but…*lads*?

"Sure!" A blush appeared on Rhianna's cream and freckled complexion. "There's a whole squad of 'em over here—from Denmark, I think. They're all blond and rugged, and I'm sure half of 'em are called Thor."

"Thor?" Beatrice intoned drily.

"Or Erik." Rhianna struck what she guessed was meant to be a Viking pose, waved away Bea's disbelief, then adroitly twisted one of the male doctors' shaving mirrors to her advantage, lowering her eyelids to half-mast to receive a whoosh of eyeshadow as she continued her story. "They're up here on some sort of epic paragliding trip, or some such. One of them was in earlier today. He had a right old bash on his thigh from where he'd landed on some gravel instead of the meadow he'd been aiming for."

She gave a swift eye roll. Clearly the injury hadn't stood in the way of a bit of flirtation.

"Either way, they're all down at the piazza and looking mad keen for some company, if you get my drift. A couple of the chalet girls and I are going to play Eeny-Meeny-Miny-Mo!" Her eyebrows did a swift little jig as a naughty grin appeared on her lips. "I'll tell you what, Dr. Jesolo. They're a right handsome bunch of lads. If there's any left over, I'll be sure to keep one for you when I come back in."

Despite herself, Bea laughed. She'd never really been that boy crazy, but she certainly remembered the giddy feeling of looking forward to a night out…the swirls of frisson…the nineteen trips to her wardrobe to make sure she'd put on just the right skirt or blouse or dress, only to turn away from the mirror and start all over again.

With Jamie it had never really been like that, it had just been…*easy*. Sure, she'd wanted to look her best, her sexiest, her most desirable, but he'd always had a remarkable way of making her feel beautiful. Even at the end of a day's long shift, when her hair had been all topsy-turvy, her makeup long gone and the shadows under her eyes had predicted a need for lots of sleep.

Quickly she finished tying her shoe and pressed herself up from the bench.

A bit too quickly as a hit of dizziness swamped her.

"Whoa! You all right there, girl?" Rhianna swooped in and steadied her. "You've not been out on the lash, have you?"

"No." Bea shrugged herself away from her colleague, trying her best not to look ungrateful. "Just got up a bit too quickly, that's all."

"Would you like me to get you some water or anything? A wee lie-down before I head off?"

"No." Bea shook her head firmly. "Absolutely not. Off you go. Have a good night, all right?"

Rhianna tipped her head to the side, her multicolored eye shadow on full display as she gave Bea a sidelong glance. "You're absolutely sure?"

"Absolutely sure about what?"

Both women turned sharply as the door to the locker room swung open.

Bea's heart swooped, then cinched tight.

One glimpse into those familiar green eyes told her she might be better off saying no.

"Dr. Jesolo here's a lifesaver!" Rhianna jumped in.

"Oh?"

If she'd thought Jamie had flinched at the sight of her he was showing no signs of any discomfort now. Just the cool reserve of a man who…

Wait a minute.

"Aren't you meant to be off tonight?" Rhianna veered off topic. "*And* you?" She wheeled around, her index finger wiggling away as if she were divining water instead of looking for answers. "What are the two of you doing here when the whole of Torpisi is out celebrating the longest day of the year?"

Collectively they reacted as a huge boom of fireworks sounded in the distance. Well, not Jamie. He was still frozen in the doorway, as if someone had sucked every last inch of joy out of him. *Terrific.* No guessing that her turning up for a few hours of burying her head in the sand had ruined his own plan to do the exact same thing.

Great minds…*per carita*!

Rhianna was the first to recover, pulling a sky blue pashmina out of her locker and swirling it around her shoulders. "Dr. Jesolo—this is your last chance. I'm telling you it's good *craic* out there."

"Craic?" Nice to have a reason to look away from Jamie. She hadn't known how powerful his not-happy glare was before.

A shard of guilt pierced through his skull. *Because you didn't bother to stick around.*

"Sure, you know good *craic* when you see it, Bea. A party. A good time—fun."

She took a quick glance between the two of them, clearly immune to the thick band of what-the-heck-are-you-doing-here? thrumming between them.

"What with Dr. Coutts being here when I guess he doesn't have to be they can spare you, sure? This is grand. You don't have to cover me at all—right, Dr. Coutts? You're all right here, aren't you? Happy to let the lovely ladies go out for a wee bit of gallivanting?"

Rhianna looked up to Jamie, seemingly undaunted by his unchanged expression. And then, just like that, it brightened.

"What a delightful idea." He unleashed a warm smile on Rhianna. One of those smiles Bea had used to get when she'd suggested they either stay on at the hospital for a couple of extra hours, just to talk through some cases, or go to bed early.

Ouch.

"Don't let me stand in the way of some gallivanting. Just the thing for a pair of young maidens on Midsummer Day."

"That's exactly what I was saying." Rhianna turned to Bea, arms crossed over her generous bosom with an I-told-you-so expression on her face. "C'mon, girl. What's the point of being up here in this rural idyll if you don't run into the arms of a Viking?"

"Oh, it's Vikings tonight, is it, Rhianna?" Jamie dropped her a playful wink, clearly no stranger to the young doctor's quest for a summer romance. Or seven. "Please. Feel free to go, Dr. Jesolo. We've got more than enough staff. Unless you were hoping for an early night?"

Bea opened her mouth to protest, then clamped it tight shut again. Where she should have felt a sting of hurt that Jamie was trying to get rid of her, she decided to take up the gauntlet from another direction. She wasn't the only one who'd told a fib in order to burn off some energy at the clinic.

"Actually, I was really looking forward to a few hours here. Special research on a—" she quickly sought a reason from the ether "—on a dissertation I'm writing."

"A dissertation?" Disbelief oozed from Rhianna's response. "What are you wasting time writing a dissertation on when you could be having fun? Isn't that the point of working up here?"

Bea's gaze flicked from Rhianna to Jamie. No way was she getting cornered into going out for a bit of *fun*!

Um...wait a minute.

"Dr. Coutts?" A nurse stuck her head in the doorway. "We've got someone I think you should see right away."

"I'll go." Bea pulled on her white coat, ignoring Rhianna's plaintive sigh and mumblings about leading horses to water—or something like that anyway—and swept past Jamie.

But not before getting a full lungful of Northern-British sexpot disguised as a surly doctor. *Humph!* She'd have to start holding her breath when she passed him from now on.

"I'm pretty certain *I* was the doctor requested."

Jamie was matching Beatrice step for step as she hotfooted it toward the waiting room.

"It doesn't matter, really," the nurse said, jogging a bit to keep up with the pair of them. "It's a lady. Midthirties, I'm guessing. She's presenting with severe gastrointestinal pain. I just thought—"

"I'll get it."

Jamie and Beatrice spoke in tandem, each with a hand on the swinging doors leading to the waiting room, their eyes blazing with undisguised sparks of frustration.

"What shall I tell the patient?" asked the befuddled nurse.

"Tell her I'll see her."

Again they spoke as one.

And then, as quickly as the fire had flared between them it shape-shifted into laughter at the ridiculousness of it all.

"You go ahead." Jamie swept a hand in the direction of the waiting room.

"No, really, I'm fine—"

A scream of pain roared past the double doors, jarring them out of their increasingly ridiculous standoff.

"Two heads are better than one?"

Jamie enjoyed the spark of recognition in Beatrice's eyes at his roundabout invitation to join him. It had been his oft-used excuse for pulling her into a consultation back at Northern General.

The adage still held true, and immediately dissolved any tension between them.

When they pushed into the room a flame-haired woman was staggering from a chair, one hand clamped to her back, one clutching her stomach. "Please help me! I can't stand it any longer!"

"Right you are, madam—oops!" Jamie swept under one of her arms, only just stopping her from falling to the ground.

"I want to lie down!" the woman howled. "Or crawl. Or *something*. Just make it stop!"

From her accent he could tell she was North American. There was a wedding ring on her finger. The flesh was puffed up around it. It looked like swelling. Water retention?

A quick glimpse down and he saw shiny white tennis shoes on her feet. The American tourist telltale. Not Canadian, then. He'd keep his maple syrup and moose jokes to himself.

"She had some of those cheese-stuffed flowers." A rusty-haired man with the most remarkable sky blue eyes rushed over from the desk, where he had been filling out some paperwork. "Marilee, honey, I *told* you not to try the flowers. They're probably hallucinogenic."

"Do you mean the pumpkin flowers?" Beatrice asked gently.

"Jesse, I'm going to *kill* you for making me try those things—ooh! Make. It. *Stop!*" She doubled over again and her husband tucked himself under her other arm.

"Those are the ones," Jesse said, sending quick looks to Jamie and Beatrice, his gaze taking on a dreamy aspect as he continued to speak. "They were deep-fried. Filled with some sort of soft cheese and a truffled honey. We were at the *enoteca*. The one up at the top of the chairlift. Have you been there?"

He looked at Beatrice, who shook her head and gave him a rueful smile before looking behind her—presumably for a wheelchair.

"I'll tell you… I thought they were delicious. I'm Joseph, by the way, though Marilee here calls me Jesse. Her very own Jesse James," he continued with a laugh, giving a quick squeeze to Beatrice's arm, seemingly oblivious to his wife's pain. He let go to shoot a pair of invisible revolvers, only just catching his wife as she stumbled and unleashed another despairing howl.

"I'll get a wheelchair," Beatrice said in a low voice to Jamie.

Jamie nodded, then stopped her with a hand on her elbow as she turned to go. "Make it a gurney." He glanced around until he found the nurse who'd signed the woman in. "Name?"

"Marilee James."

"All right, Marilee. We're just going to get you—oops! Easy, there, I've got you. Over this way, love."

Beatrice had magicked a gurney out of the ether and was already pushing it through the waiting room door.

"Now, if I can just get my colleague to…" He flicked his eyes from Bea to Marilee, which, true to form, Beatrice understood as "Come over here and help me get her up on the gurney because the husband's not much use."

After a handful of awkward maneuvers, the sturdy but fit-looking woman was up and on the gurney.

"Mrs. James—"

"Call me Marilee. I can't stand the formal stuff... *Ooo-eee...* It hurts. Do you think it was the clams, Jesse?" She reached back and grabbed her husband's hand as he tried to keep up with the moving gurney, squeezing it until it was white. "We should never have had seafood up here in the mountains. This is *not* the vacation of my dreams you promised!"

"I know, my little cherry pie. But we'll get it right. I'm sure they have loads of medication they can give you here for the pain." He shot anxious looks in Jamie's direction as he pulled the gurney.

They did. But only if they knew what was going on.

"Have you been sick at all? Vomiting, diarrhea?" Jamie tipped his head toward an open exam area. "Let's get her in there for an abdominal exam. Can you call up to X-ray? We might need a—"

Marilee's scream drowned out his instructions to Beatrice, who stood, calm as she always was in a crisis. He could almost see the medical terminology whizzing past her eyes as her mind did its usual high-speed race through possible prognoses.

"She hasn't been sick," said Jessie. "Not at all. And we only had the clams about half an hour ago. Lovely, they were. All sorts of garlic and some kinda green thingy. A little chopped-up herb."

"Appendicitis?"

Jamie threw the word softly to Beatrice, who nodded one of those could-be nods and then parried with a whispered "Spleen?"

"No, it wasn't that. Something more like parsley, but Italian-style. Mountain grass?" Jesse looked to his wife, who answered him with an I-don't-know glare.

"Are you having any trouble passing wind, Mrs.—Marilee?"

As if to prove she wasn't, the woman rolled to the side and rather dramatically passed a healthy gust of wind.

Beatrice turned to Jamie and rather spectacularly managed a straight face as she said, "Perhaps passing wind isn't the trouble after all. Can you tell us where the feeling is most acute, Marilee?"

She put a hand on the woman's belly, doing her best to work around the fact Marilee seemed unable to remain stationary for more than a few seconds.

"My back!" Marilee plunged a hand behind her and then quickly grabbed one of Jamie's hands and one of Beatrice's and dragged them to the center of her belly, pulling her knees up to her stomach as she did so. "Oh, my sweet blazes. It's wet. I feel *wet*! Am I bleeding?"

Jamie shot Beatrice a worried look. This was more than a case of gastroenteritis.

"Pseudocyesis?" Beatrice whispered, tucking her shoulders down and dropping a quick shrug.

False pregnancy was a far reach, but…

"Psuedo *what*? Don't bother whispering. Little Bat Ears, my Jesse calls me." Marilee tightened her grip on Jamie's hand.

"That's right, my little sugar pie." Jesse beamed from the far end of the gurney, his eyes suddenly widening. "Oh, my blue-blooded ancestors! Marilee, your dress is all wet."

"Marilee?" Jamie quickly untucked his hand from hers, seeing the situation for what it was in an instant. "Why didn't you tell us you were pregnant?"

"Uh..." Jesse held up his hands—minus the invisible pistols this time—and started backing up. "Hang on there a minute, Doc. My Marilee may be a lot of things. But pregnant is most certainly *not* one of them."

Marilee pushed herself up on her elbows and shot wild-eyed looks between each doctor, her cheeks pinkening as the rest of her face paled.

"Let's get you lying back down here—all right, Marilee." Jamie moved to the side of the gurney, gently pressing on the woman's shoulders and only losing eye contact to indicate to Beatrice that she should do a vaginal exam.

Beatrice quickly shifted down to the foot of the gurney, snapping on a pair of gloves as she went, and deftly blocked Jesse's view.

After a surreptitious glimpse, and the most infinitesimal of nods to Jamie to tell him that he'd made the right call, she turned to Mr. Jesse James and began to guide him to a chair adjacent to his wife's gurney.

Jamie replaced Beatrice, barely containing his astonishment at what he saw. Thank goodness

Beatrice had stayed behind. He'd need someone who could keep their head on their shoulders for this one.

"How're your midwifery skills, Dr. Jesolo?"

"All right." Beatrice threw a look over her shoulder as she gowned up.

Jamie grinned. "That's good. Because Mrs. James is crowning."

"What the heck are you people on about?" Marilee cut in. "I just ate some funny cheesy flowers, is all!"

"Marilee, I think you'd better lie back and ask your husband if you can hold his hand." Jamie kept his voice as calm as possible. "It looks like the pair of you are about to become parents."

He shot a look over to Beatrice, who was popping on a fresh pair of gloves and unfurling a disposable surgical gown.

"Doctor?" Bea held out the gown for him.

He swiftly stepped into the gown and for one brief moment their gazes caught and meshed as if they were back at Northern General. Madly in love. Meeting challenge after challenge with dexterity and skill.

And that was when she knew she had never—not for one second—stopped loving him.

"There is no chance at all there is a baby inside me," Marilee was busy explaining. "We've been married over eighteen years. Exchanged rings the first day we were legal, then spent the next seventeen trying to have a baby. Isn't that right, Jesse? Then last year we decided to give up. It was just going to be you and me. Why, I think the last time we—"

She stopped midsentence and reached out for her husband's hand.

"Do you remember the last time *before* the last time? Not last night's last time, but the *other* last time?"

"Sugar bean, I don't know what you're talking about—unless you mean the last time we—oh… Do you mean…the whipped cream night?"

"Mmm-hmm… Thanksgiving?" She teased the memory up a bit more, her voice dipping an octave, to a lower, more sultry tone, saying something about pumpkin pie and cinnamon-hot spices before lurching back up with a sharply pitched gasp.

As hard as she tried, Bea couldn't contain the

crazy feeling of sisterhood she felt with Marilee. Against all the odds, the American woman was going to have a child!

She'd be doing the same in a few months' time. Granted, she'd be on her own—Jamie wouldn't be there, asking if she'd eaten bad clams, and there would be the press to contend with eventually because she wouldn't be able to hide away forever—but…a *baby*! The explosive joy of it warmed her chest and recharged her, as if she'd just woken up from a perfect night's sleep.

"You're going to be all right, Marilee. If you thought about this for seventeen years, you'll have read a fair few books on what to expect."

Wide-eyed, Marilee looked up, panting through a hit of pain and doing her best to nod.

"I've read 'em all. And nearly each one of them mentioned getting painkillers. That's all I was hoping for when we came stumbling in here. Just a couple of pills to take the edge off and then we were going to get back for the rest of the fireworks—weren't we, honey bun?"

"Sure were, sugar bee. Now, look what you've done! Thrown everything all off-kilter. We're going to miss the grand finale."

"I think you two are going to have one exciting grand finale of your own to the evening," Jamie said. "You're fully dilated, Marilee. This baby's going to be here in the next few minutes."

Bea glanced across at him, enjoying the warmth of his smile. She knew he loved babies every bit as much as she did. He hadn't been the least bit shy about telling her he hoped to be a father to a fleet of little ones.

It wouldn't be fair to ask...

"Dr. Coutts, are you sure you're seeing everything straight? Are you *positive* it's a baby?"

Bea had to stem a rush of emotion as Marilee's voice caught and grew jagged as she well and truly began to take on board how enormous a turn her life was about to take.

"How could you not have known?" Jesse threw up his hands. "I thought you were meant to throw up or go off your favorite foods or something?"

"I most certainly did no such thing," Marilee shot back indignantly, then went quiet. "Or did I…? I can't remember. Maybe after those oysters on Valentine's Day, but… Jesse James!" She threw the argument back at her husband. "How could *you* not have noticed? Aren't men supposed to be fine-tuned to a woman's breasts getting bigger or something?"

She shot Bea a glance to garner some support for her argument. The best Bea could come up with was a who-knows? face. This was her first surprise pregnancy. She'd certainly heard about them, but… Well, everything about her own pregnancy had been planned down to the microsecond.

Not so much a surprise as a secret… Even if her ex-fiancé had held out until the wedding, he probably would have run for the hills once the baby was born. Perhaps his infertility was nature's way of stating the obvious. The man wasn't meant to be a father. Just as well, he'd hit the road before they'd had to worry about divorce proceedings.

Bea smiled as Marilee grabbed her, then tightened her grip on her hand, pulling her in for a stage-whispered "At least he knows it's his."

"How could I not, my little sugar plum pie? That Thanksgiving dinner was the best…" He looked up to the sky, swiped at the beads of sweat accruing on his forehead. "That was a real doozy."

"I sure do love you, Jesse." Marilee's eyes filled with tears.

"I love you, too, Marilee. There isn't a single other woman on the planet I would have a child with just when I thought we'd have the whole rest of our lives to play."

"You mean—" Marilee's eyes widened. "I guess this *does* take the cliff-jumping trip to Mexico off the agenda for a while."

"We'll get through it, Marilee." Jesse tipped his head down and dropped a kiss on his wife's forehead. "We always do."

As the scene unfolded Bea was finding it harder to keep a check on her emotions. Her family wasn't one of those so-called traditional European families—lavishing each other with kisses and bear hugs and the smother-love Italian mothers in particular were renowned for. Jamie's was. Open arms. Broad, unaffected smiles. Unfettered affection…

All the light she'd felt about her own pregnancy abruptly disappeared into a deep pool of fears.

She'd be a single mother.

Alone.

Her mother was the last person on earth she'd go to for advice. Her nanny would be a better source of wisdom than—

No!

She was going to do this.

But it's scary.

She had to do this.

All on your own.

Bea took a surreptitious glance at the couple, now reaching for each other's hands, trying to grasp the magnitude of what was happening to them, and felt a pure bolt of envy rocket through her.

She could have had this. Maybe not the surprise labor part—but she could have had this with Jamie. She hadn't been sure, but something had told her Jamie had wanted to ask her to marry him. They'd walked past that beautiful old stone house, paused and daydreamed enough times. It would have needed so much work…

"Here you are, Jesse. Why don't you keep your wife's forehead cool with this cloth? And, Marilee? Perhaps we should get a pillow under your head, there."

Bea huffed out a sigh, trying her best to disguise it as a reaction to the misstep she took as she turned away, no longer able to remain neutral as the couple began to shed tears of joy as the news sank in.

She'd misstepped, all right.

In so many ways.

She was—what was it now?—ten weeks along and not one person had noticed a single change in her. Not that there was anything dramatic this early on, but even so… Her breasts were a bit bigger than when she'd first found out. And though she hated to admit it, she was going to have to do some internet-shopping pretty quickly to get some bigger pants.

Bea glanced at Jamie, quietly, deftly at work, sliding a pair of stirrups down from the end of the multipurpose gurney. She knew it was crazy to look to him for reactions to this pregnancy that had clearly taken this pair by surprise, but she couldn't help wondering what Jamie would think if he found out *she* was pregnant. Keeping it secret had seemed the best thing at the time. The wisest thing. If he were to know, would he—

No. No, he wouldn't. And, no, you shouldn't,

Bea silently chastised herself, before realigning her focus to Marilee.

"How about slipping your feet in these, love?" Jamie eased her tennis shoes off, then carefully slipped each foot into a stirrup.

Marilee grinned and giggled at the instruction, and then quickly her features crumpled in agony as another contraction hit. It was a sign for Bea not to get hopeful. She wasn't pregnant with Jamie's baby. And that simple fact made a world of difference.

"You've got a lot to answer for, Jesse James," Marilee hollered, in between biting down on her lip and doing her best to mimic Bea as she started to show her how to control her breath.

"Nice and steady, there, Marilee." She glanced across at Jamie, who gave her a nod. "You ready to start pushing?"

Sweat was trickling from the poor woman's brow. This was a lot of information to take in at once. A dream vacation turning into a—a dream baby? It was definitely the last souvenir the couple had anticipated bringing home from their European journey.

"Shall I get that cloth back in the cool water for you, Jesse?"

"You can get my wife some drugs, is what you can do," Jesse asserted, as if he'd been recalling a TV medical drama and remembering it was *his* turn to demand an epidural.

Jamie, having spread a paper cloth over Marilee's knees, was taking another look. "I'm afraid we're a bit too far along for any painkillers."

"We?" Marilee barked, trying once again to elbow herself up to a seated position. "We are talking about *me*, and *I* think it is high time you gave me some!"

"Breathe. Remember to breathe, Marilee. Just a couple more pushes and we're there."

Jamie ducked behind the blue paper towel, his hand already on the crowning head of the little one. Beatrice had wrapped her hands around Marilee's and was breathing along with her, murmuring words of encouragement.

Every bit of him longed to look across at those dark brown eyes of hers. Share a complicit smile. Revel in all that was yet to come for these soon-to-be-parents. But today was yet another vivid reminder that none of that would be coming for *him*. Falling in love again would be a big enough miracle, let alone having a family with someone who wasn't Beatrice.

"It stings! Really, *really* stings!" Marilee managed through her deep breaths.

"That's a normal sensation to feel. Especially without any painkillers." Jamie put up a hand to stop Marilee's knees from catching his head in a clamp. Given the madness of the situation, it probably would be fitting.

"Can't you give her *anything*?" Jesse was throwing panicked looks between him and his wife, whose face was scrunching up as she bore down for another push. "Gas? Ether? Knock her out with something? I can't stand to see my little sweet honey bear in so much pain!"

"Oh, no—we wouldn't want her to go to sleep now…" Jamie's jaw tensed as he cupped one hand beneath the baby's emerging head.

"Why the hell not? She's in *agony*!"

Jamie's own features tightened as Marilee's scream of primal pain reached epic proportions. Within seconds he was helping the rest of the little form wriggle free, uncoiling the tiniest bit of umbilical cord from its foot, tipping it back to prevent any blood or amniotic fluid from going into his lungs.

And, yes, Beatrice was there, as if he'd summoned her out loud. The same rhythm. The same ability to read his mind. No matter what chaos reigned between the pair of them on a personal level, he knew he could rely on her to be one hundred percent professional.

She gave the baby's mouth and nose a quick suction with a bulb syringe, and then, with the umbilical cord still attached, he reached across and laid the now-crying child on his mother's stomach.

"And miss the birth of your son…"

The Jameses gasped in disbelief, their eyes clouding with tears as they took in the sight of their red-haired son.

"Jesse Junior," Jesse whispered, tickling the tip of his son's teensy nose with his index finger.

"Jesse Walton Junior," Marilee added with an equally starry-eyed expression, her finger teasing at the clutch of fingers making up her son's miniature fist.

"J. W. Junior. My little boy."

As the couple carried on with their cooing, Jamie quickly clamped the umbilical cord, while Beatrice gave the baby a bit of a wipe to clear some of the vernix from his skin. Jamie could hear her agreeing, that, yes, he was the cutest baby she'd ever seen and, no, she'd never been through anything like this before. Yes, she *did* think he weighed enough, and he *was* long enough. She answered all the questions as calmly as if she'd done this a thousand times before, and as joyfully as if she'd never before experienced the magic of seeing a newborn.

He delivered the placenta and made sure his patient was clear of any cuts or tears.

"Not a one?" Jesse exclaimed, all the while giving his wife the thumbs-up. "That's my girl!"

Bea magicked the baby away to weigh and measure him, and put a little tag on his wrist—even though they had no obstetrics ward in the small clinic, so he would most likely be their only newborn tonight and there was no one to mix him up with.

A hit of longing struck him so suddenly when Beatrice reentered the exam area, holding the swaddled baby in her arms, that he had to turn away. She would see right through him.

Pulling in a draught of air, he swallowed back the sharp sting of emotion. That micromoment couldn't have been more pronounced. He could have sliced each second into a hundred frames. A glimpse into what fatherhood would feel like. Pride. Unchecked love. A bit of fear as to whether he would be able to do the best by his child—and its mother…

He forced himself to turn around again, only to clash and connect again with Beatrice's dark-eyed gaze. She hadn't moved. Had frozen on the spot as if the moment had been as laden with emotion for her as it had for him.

He felt as if his chest was being crushed, and his heart was barely able to provide the simple pumping action required to keep him alive… Because without Beatrice in his life…

Jesse was walking across the room to retrieve his son. Jamie barely noticed when he elbowed him out of the way.

"Now, you just hand that little whippersnapper over here, Dr. Jesolo. Daddy and Mommy are going to take care of him now."

Bea looked up, her dark lashes beaded with tears, her sole focus on Jamie.

"So…" Jesse looked between the pair of them, "What about the two of you, huh?"

Jamie cleared his throat, tore his gaze away from Beatrice, forcing himself to face reality. "What *about* us?"

"When are you two going to have a child?" Marilee joined in, arms extended toward her husband to regain possession of her newborn.

Jamie hadn't meant to laugh. The idea had been far from ridiculous at one point in their lives. But now? *No.* Children weren't on the menu.

He glanced across at Beatrice, who had backed up against the curtain, her expression stricken as if the question had caught her completely off guard.

Marilee's brow crinkled. "You're obviously together, or you wouldn't have been shooting all those doe-eyed looks at one another when the baby came out, wouldja?"

"Oh, no." Beatrice pulled the curtain back and took another step away from Jamie. "We're not… We're not a couple."

"No!" Jamie shook his head and popped on a smile, as if people were always honing in on the fact that he was just pals with the woman who had smashed his heart into smithereens.

I messed that up a long time ago.

"If you'll excuse me? I'm just going to get a vitamin-K jab for your little one."

When the Jameses raised their eyebrows in alarm he assured them it was standard practice. Nothing to worry about.

When he headed out into the corridor there was no sign of Beatrice.

Being with her, watching her hold that tiny child in her arms was as close a glimpse as he'd get to believing he and Beatrice could start again.

Yes, they had history. And there was a part of him that wasn't sure he'd entirely forgiven her for leaving. Or forgiven himself for breaking his Hippocratic oath by getting too close to his patients. Too emotionally involved.

Which was exactly what he was doing right now. Superimposing someone else's emotions onto his own hollowed-out heart.

He might be able to forgive Beatrice for leaving, but how would he ever be able to trust that she wouldn't do it again? Pick up and leave when her mother unearthed another prince or far-off royal for her to wed in order to uphold the di Jesolo name?

More important… He needed to stop pointing the finger of blame.

He'd had a chance to fight for his true love and he hadn't done it. Had just stood back and watched it happen.

He *deserved* this. Deserved the searing heartache. The bleak, unfulfilling future as a bachelor… The single bed. The sleepless nights. All in a vainglorious attempt to escape the wretched truth.

He had let her go.

Let her walk out of his life as if she hadn't meant a thing.

It wasn't his place to forgive. He saw that now. It was hers.

CHAPTER EIGHT

"AT LAST!" TEO pulled his head in from the window. "This must be the first day without rain in—what?—a fortnight?"

"Something like that. It's not been the best of summers, has it?"

Jamie gave Teo a clap on the shoulder, before turning around and nearly careening into Beatrice as she went out to the waiting room to fetch a patient.

"Apologies!" He raised his hands and backed off, trying his best to ignore her sidelong look as she slipped through the swinging doors, leaving a trail of fresh linen and honey in her wake.

They might have called a truce, but polite chitchat wasn't making working with Beatrice any easier. If anything, the surprise-baby night had only made him more aware of just how singular a woman she was. An amazing doctor. Kind and generous. Calm in a crisis. Quieter than he remembered her being back in England, when her laughter had been able to bring a room to life. Still every bit as beautiful.

It didn't help that she had taken to life in the village as naturally as dewdrops to a flower petal. She had well and truly blossomed in the past few weeks. There was a lovely pink bloom to her cheeks, and a…a softness about her that complemented her slender figure.

He scribbled out a prescription for a patient he'd just seen—a regular at the clinic owing to his severe asthma, who'd had the temerity to scrunch his face up when he saw Jamie was going to be the doctor and asked for Beatrice instead.

"Such a lovely young woman. Don't you think so, Dr. Coutts?"

The cheek! He'd been there for a year and had yet to have *anyone* request him. Then again… he hadn't exactly been himself. Before or after she'd arrived. And no doubt he'd be a right old curmudgeon when she left. There was no winning at this game.

"Dr. Coutts?" Rhianna held out a tablet to him so he could check another patient's stats.

Jamie started. He'd been staring at Beatrice. *Again.*

"Yes...good." He scanned the stats. "I think she's good to go. Can you give her a couple of extra ice packs for the journey back to the campsite?"

"Will do." Rhianna nodded with a smile. "And Dr. Coutts...?"

Jamie turned away from staring at the platinum blond pixie cut, astonished at how short his attention span was. "Yes—sorry?"

"It's good to see you in—" her eyes traveled over toward Bea "—in such good spirits."

She gave her eyebrows a little happy jig and tossed him a knowing wink as she rejoined the mother and teenage daughter trying out new crutches in the wake of a freshly sprained ankle.

Jamie gave his face a scrub. Was he that transparent? He knew he hadn't been able to hide it at Northern General. Hadn't felt any need. He'd been in love.

He tried shrugging it off. Just because Rhianna was having a torrid summer romance with one of the adventure-tour-group guides it didn't mean every single person in the clinic needed to be floating on air. Someone had to keep his feet firmly grounded. He was *British*! Made of stern stuff. He could make it through the summer without falling in love again. As sure as the sun would hit the horizon every day of the week, he could keep himself emotionally off-limits.

He forced himself to focus on the patients board until, a few minutes later, he found himself unable to drown out the sound of a crying baby.

He turned and saw a mother handing her infant over to Beatrice, who expertly tucked the baby into her hands using *his* "magic trick." The special hold he'd been taught by his mentor that never failed to stop a baby from crying.

Fold the right and then left arm across the child's chest, use an index finger to prop up the little chin and tip the child to a forty-five-degree angle. Place your other hand along its nappy and rock it. A bit like a baby jig, but gently. Slowly. And in… That's right… In just a few seconds a smiley, relaxed baby.

He vividly remembered teaching Beatrice the technique. The light in her eyes when she'd had a success on her first try.

Beatrice looked up, perhaps feeling the weight of his gaze upon her?

And when their eyes met…

Lightning strike.

It never failed to amaze him.

Bea's gaze dropped to the child for just a moment before she returned it to meet his eyes, and in that instant of reconnection he saw something in her he hadn't seen before. Was it—longing for a *child*?

As quickly as their gazes had clicked and meshed, Beatrice's attention was straight back on the mother, discussing the reason for their visit. A rash on the infant's leg, from the looks of things.

"Dr. Coutts?" A nurse was holding out a phone for him as Beatrice disappeared behind the curtain of her cubicle. "You've got a call from 118."

His pulse quickened. The Italian mountain-rescue team.

"This is Dr. Coutts. What's the situation?"

He listened silently as the caller detailed an accident. An accident involving a school group on holiday from England. A massive landslide. A bus. Crushed roof.

Regular medics were en route in the helicopter, but they needed ground crews because of the number of children involved. The fire department was on their way, too, but they needed more medical personnel. Did they have anyone free?

He glanced up at the clock. It was late afternoon. They'd have a few hours of daylight left, and they were precious.

"We've got another shift coming in a couple of hours. For now I can get together a team of three or four. More to follow."

It would have to do.

He quickly called one of the ambulance drivers on the radio to come and meet them at the clinic entrance.

When he turned around Beatrice was waving off her patients—a happy mother and a giggling baby.

"Dr. Jesolo, can you suit up for an emergency rescue?"

If she wasn't keen to participate, she didn't let it show. Just nodded and headed off to the supplies area. A true professional.

"Dr. Brandisi?" He flicked his thumb in the

direction Beatrice was heading. "Suit up. We've got a long night ahead."

Teo gave him a quick, grim nod, finished up with his patient and the pair of them headed off to change.

"Steel yourself," Jamie warned Teo—the most anxious and excited father-to-be he had ever encountered. "This one's full of children."

"Children?" Bea had caught the end of Jamie's warning as she tugged on a red jumpsuit. "What age?"

"A group of eight-year-olds, I think. Hiking holiday. Wilderness skills or something. About twenty-plus counsellors and a few parents."

Jamie's expression was flinty. A sure sign that he was steeling himself from the inside out for the worst-case scenario.

If there was any time she needed to keep her emotions at bay, it was now. Carrying a precious life inside her had not only ramped up her hormones, it had opened up her heart in a way she hadn't imagined possible. As if carrying a child herself had made her a proxy mother to every other child she encountered until she could hold her own beautiful baby in her arms.

"Fatalities?"

Jamie gave a sharp nod. "Definitely the driver. Thrown through the front window on impact. Lacerate carotid." He huffed out a tight breath. "We should get an update on our way up there. Have you all got your run bags?"

Teo shouldered his large emergency travel bag and picked up Bea's bag with his free hand.

"Don't worry—I can get that." She didn't want special treatment. Not yet anyway.

Teo gave her a look. One that said she hadn't been hiding her pregnancy symptoms as well as she thought she had. "I'll carry it to the ambo. When we get there you're on your own. But call me if you need anything. No heavy lifting, all right?"

She glanced across at Jamie, relieved to see he was busy rattling through a list of medications they'd require in addition to what was already on the emergency vehicle.

"Is he..." Teo began, eyes gone double wide with disbelief.

"No!" Bea shushed him as quickly as she could. "Just—I need this job, all right?"

She pulled her fingers across her lips in a zip-it-up-pal move, but not in time to stop Jamie catching the end of it.

The vertical furrows between his eyes deepened. "Everything all right with you two? This is going to be intense. We don't have time for any disputes between colleagues."

"No, mate." Teo stepped forward, all business. "We're all good here. Just trying to be chivalrous and it got Dr. Jesolo's dander up a bit—didn't it, Bea?"

He turned and gave her a complicit wink. He'd be quiet. *For now.*

Which was just as well because she knew the coming hours were going to be tough.

The minutes of their ride to the accident ticked past in a merciless silence. Each doctor was shoring up their emotional and mental reserves as information began trickling in on the ambulance driver's radio.

Bea felt as though mere seconds had passed

when the ambulance lurched to a stop and they opened up the back.

Cars were already backed up along the narrow mountain route—the only way to the summer resort at the foot of the Alpine glacier. And up beyond there was some hastily put-up emergency tape.

Bea could see the fire crew already on-site, and heard the loud, shrill screech of metal on metal reverberating against the exposed chunk of the mountainside laid bare by the devastating landslide.

Each shouldering their emergency packs, the three doctors took off at a steady jog to reach the overturned bus, precariously hanging to the cliffside. When they arrived, Jamie led them to the head of the 118 team.

"Dr. Coutts, good to have you on-site." The man stepped forward and gave him a quick handshake. "We've got to shoot off with two of the most critically injured patients. Will you be all right taking charge?"

Jamie nodded. "Anything in place yet?"

"Only the triage sites. I'll leave assignments up to you. We've kicked off with START." He glanced over at the helicopter, its rotors already beginning to whirr into action.

"START?" Bea looked to Jamie. She wasn't familiar with the acronym.

"Simple triage and rapid treatment." He nodded across to a lay-by near the bus, where large plastic ground cloths in bright colors had been laid out. "Red, yellow, green and black. Critical, observation, minor or walking wounded, and expectant."

"Expectant?" Bea gave a little stomp of frustration. What a time for her English to be failing her.

"Deceased or expected to die," Jamie said, his green eyes following a pair of fire crew members carrying an adult-sized body bag over to the black tarp. He looked back to Bea, concern tightening his features. "It's harsh, but essential if we're going to get to those who require critical care."

"I'll help with the crew tagging up at the bus—all right, Doc?" Teo took off at a run when he received Jamie's okay.

"Let us know if you need a hand," he called after him, and then placed a solid hand on Bea's shoulder. "Are you up to this? Do you want me to get someone else on board?"

"No. Absolutely not."

She shook her head clear of the fog of information overload. No matter how distant he'd been over the past few weeks, she took strength from his touch now. From knowing he was there. If she ever wanted anyone at an emergency situation it would be Jamie. The calm at the eye of any storm.

"Where would you like me?"

"Are you up for the critically wounded? I'll be there. Working between you and Teo."

She nodded. Despite everything, she knew she flourished at work with Jamie by her side.

"Let's get to it."

"I need an extra pair of hands over here!"

Jamie called across to Beatrice, who was downgrading a child she had resuscitated to the yellow crew. Another life saved.

"What have you got?" She was there in an instant.

He glanced across at her as she knelt on the other side of the young boy he was tending to, relieved to see the hesitation he'd noticed in her when they'd arrived had completely vanished. She was one hundred percent focused now. Exactly what the situation warranted.

And then she saw it. The long shaft of thin metal impaling the boy in the lower part of his chest. She glanced up at the boy's face, her eyes widening, then quickly regrouped into a smile as she felt the boy's gaze on her.

"Well, look at what you've gone and done!" Beatrice chided the boy teasingly, her eyes not leaving his for an instant.

"It's pretty cool, isn't it?" the boy answered.

"This is Ryan." Jamie pulled a hard plastic brace out of his case. "He's got quite a few ideas about his own treatment, but first I think we need to slip a neck brace on him. What do you say, Ryan?"

The boy began to nod in agreement, then winced.

"Easy, *amore*," Beatrice cautioned. "I love your enthusiasm, but how about we keep all responses verbal rather than physical?" She held eye contact with the boy until she'd received an okay and a smile. "And is this little bit of extra equipment coming or going?" Her eyes shot to the small blood stain slowly spreading out from the wound on the front of his T-shirt. Ryan had yet to spot it.

"It's one of the tent poles," Ryan volunteered shakily. "I was holding the tent kit in my seat so I could be ready to set up camp."

"You sound like me when I was in the Scouts." Jamie smiled at the memory of his escapades in the woods. When being a child was all that he'd had to worry about.

"I'm not a Scout," Ryan corrected. "I'm a wilderness expert! If my leg's broken, we can pull out this tent pole and break it in two and then use it as a splint. And if it grows too dark, I can start a fire with my flint stone. It's here in my pocket."

He began moving his hand toward his jeans pocket.

"Hold on there, pal. No need for fires just yet. Your leg's looking all right. Let's just try to stay as still as possible, okay, Ryan?" Jamie laughed at the boy. "As much as I'd like to take it out, I think Dr. Jesolo will agree with me that the tent pole is probably holding more together than ripping it apart."

Beatrice gave an affirmative nod. A surge of energy heated his chest. This was what it had been like in "the good old days." A real team. Better than that. A dynamic duo.

"What would happen if you took it out?" Ryan asked after giving a disappointed sigh.

"Well..." Jamie rocked his weight back on his heels. He always had to play things carefully with his pediatric patients. Kids were smart. They liked information and they could tell when he was holding back. Then again, they were *kids* and as enthused as Ryan was, terrifying him with details about bleeding out wasn't the object of the game.

"What do you say we leave it in place until we get you to a proper OR? That way if there's any blood loss they'll be able to sort you out straightaway. In the meantime we're going to hook you up to an IV to get some fluids and a bit of pain relief running around your system. How does that sound?"

"Cool! I've always wanted to see what it was

like in an operating theater. Especially if I'm arriving in a helicopter!"

"Are you planning to be a doctor?" Beatrice asked, while Jamie began cutting away the youngster's shirt so he could get a better look.

He laughed along with her when Ryan announced that he planned to set up his own clinic in the woods to treat both humans *and* bears.

"Oops! Try your best not to move, *amore*."

Ryan's breathing shifted as they laughed, quickly becoming labored, indicating that the pole might have nicked one of his lungs. Pneumothoraxes could be fatal. But they didn't have to be.

Jamie did a quick run of stats. "Blood pressure is stable. Pulse is high."

"Not surprising, given then circumstances. When is the next helicopter due?" Beatrice asked, giving him a quick glance before they both turned to look up at the darkening sky. Dusk was just beginning to set in, and getting as many of the children out of the bus before the sun set was crucial.

"When do I get to ride in a helicopt—ow! It hurts."

"I know, mate. We're going to get you something for the pain." He looked across at Beatrice. "We can't use topical numbing agents. Can you hold on to the pole while I check if it's a through and through?"

"Me?" Ryan asked in disbelief.

"No, *amore*. I'll do that," said Beatrice. "You just concentrate on staying still. I know it's tough, but you're doing so well."

Beatrice gave Jamie a nod, indicating that she was ready, quickly folding the trauma pads he handed her in half and then placing them on either side of the metal rod.

"How many more pads do you need?"

"Are you pulling it out?" Ryan's voice was straining against the pain now.

"Not yet, Ryan." Jamie ran a hand along the boy's creased brow. "We're just seeing how far this bad boy has penetrated."

"A couple more pads, please." Beatrice held out a hand. "That should be enough to stabilize the rod up to the halfway point. Enough to turn him over and check for the through and through."

Jamie quickly handed her the extra folded

dressing pads, which she laid crossways to the layer below, gently pressing on them as Jamie slipped both his hands under the boy's side and ducked to take a quick look.

"No." He shook his head, lowering the boy as carefully as he could back to the ground. "It didn't come through."

"Aw…" Ryan lifted his hand to the tent pole but Jamie quickly trapped the small fingers in his own, pressing them firmly to the ground. He couldn't help but laugh. "Were you hoping for a through and through, pal?"

"A little…" Ryan tried lifting himself up again, and instantly started gasping for air.

"I'm just going to put this oxygen mask on you, Ryan. It should help your breathing." Beatrice lowered her voice and continued to speak, ducking her head away from Ryan's eye line to Jamie's as she did so. "Do you think the pole could've cracked any ribs on entry?"

"Tough to tell at this point. Best thing we can do is stabilize him as much as possible and get him to a hospital."

Jamie tugged his medical kit closer. He'd need to pull out the works on this one.

"Ryan?" A mother's frantic tones broke through the hum of voices. With so many children injured and receiving treatment, only a mother would be calling for one boy in particular. *"Ryan!"*

The calls began to fade as quickly as they'd risen. From the sounds of it she'd made a quick scan of the medical triage site and, having missed her son, was now working her way back toward the crash site.

Jamie pressed down on the boy's shoulders, knowing he would want to respond if it *was* his parent.

"Mum?" Ryan fought for breath to say it again—scream it—but found himself fighting for breath. Tears sprang to his eyes as he whispered, "I want my mum!"

"I know you do, mate. We'll get her, but you've got to stay put—all right?" He looked up to Beatrice. "Can you find her? Ryan? C'mon. Stay with us, mate. Can you tell me what your surname is?"

"Cooper..." Ryan's voice was barely audible as the blood began to drain from his face.

"There's swelling of the subcutaneous tissues," Beatrice said quietly.

"I'm going to have to put in a chest tube."

"Thoracotomy?" she asked.

"Needle decompression. Are you all right to find the mother?"

If he acted fast, he could get it done and restore the boy's oxygen flow. It would be less frightening for the mother to see her son with a needle and a valve in his chest than gasping for breath.

"Absolutely. I'll check on the helicopter, as well."

The low-altitude trip to the hospital might necessitate a chest drain, as well. He'd wait for Beatrice to return to put that in.

Jamie nodded his thanks, noticing as she rose, how her hands slid protectively to her stomach. It was the second or third time that day he'd seen her repeat the gesture. He wondered if she'd hurt herself—got a cut or scrape in all the frantic lifting and carrying of children from the bus to the triage tarps. Adrenaline ran so high during incidents like these it was easy enough to get injured while trying to help those in need.

She was gone before he could ask. Jamie shook

his head, turning to his medical kit to rake through his supplies. It was hardly the time to speculate on things that weren't critical medical issues. Then again, maybe his not paying attention was what had lost him Beatrice's affections in the first place.

But his not paying attention now could cost this child his life.

Jamie blinkered his vision so it was on Ryan, forcing himself to drown out all of the other stimuli whirling around them. The sirens, the crying children, the screech and scream of the fire department's Jaws of Life still extracting children from the seats that had virtually fallen like dominoes in on each other.

The fact they'd only lost the driver so far was little short of divine intervention. Three children had already been flown out to a large hospital near Milan. Ryan was the last critical case they had here. The yellow team were busy with a lot of cuts, sprains and a few broken bones. The compound fractures had already been sent off by ambulance. So it was just him and Ryan right now on helicopter watch.

He pulled on a fresh pair of gloves, and by

touch located the second intercostal space on Ryan's chest. Using his other hand, he swiped at the area with an iodine-based swab, then deftly inserted a large-bore needle just above the boy's third rib. Holding the needle perpendicular to Ryan's chest, he leaned in, listening for the telltale hissing sound of air escaping.

A sigh of relief huffed out of his own chest at the noise, and he quickly set to removing the needle, leaving the catheter in place while opening the cannula to air.

"Ryan? *Ryan!*"

Jamie looked up from securing the final piece of tape to see a woman running at full speed toward him, calling out her son's name.

Beatrice was just behind her, one hand on her belly as it had been before and the other on her back. When her eyes met Jamie's she stopped cold, her hands dropping to her sides, her expression completely horrified.

As quickly as he'd registered her dismay, it disappeared, and Beatrice joined the woman who had dropped to her knees beside her son and began answering the inevitable flood of queries, her hand slowly, but somehow inevitably, creeping to the small of her back.

A thousand questions were running through Jamie's mind and they should have all be about his patient. But every single thought in his head was building up to one shocking realization.

Beatrice was pregnant.

"The helicopter is on its way back." Bea braved looking into Jamie's eyes. "They think it'll be here in ten, maybe fifteen, minutes." Flinching at the wobble in her voice, she just prayed no one else noticed it.

"Right."

The monosyllabic answer was all the proof Bea needed.

Jamie knew. She'd seen it in his eyes. He knew she was carrying a child.

She'd been doing her best to hide the intense cramping that had hit her throughout the afternoon, but this latest bout of running must have exacerbated things. Fear suddenly gripped her. Her concentration on the injured children had been so intense she hadn't bothered connecting the dots.

She was twelve weeks pregnant now. Still within that window where miscarriage was, for many women, a constant worry. She'd never been pregnant before, so had no idea how her body would respond to pregnancy. So far it had been the typical symptoms: tender breasts, nausea and sharp hits of fatigue. She'd been careful. Or so she'd thought. Keeping her shifts at the clinic to a minimum, but regular enough so as not to raise any alarms.

"I think you will need to go with Ryan."

She only just heard Jamie through the roar of her thoughts.

"No." She shook her head solidly. "Absolutely not. His mother should go with him. There's not much room on the chopper."

"Which is why *you* should go. Mrs. Cooper…"

Bea watched as Jamie did what he did best. Calmed. Soothed.

"We can get you transported down to the hospital so that you'll be there in good time to meet him coming out of surgery."

"Oh, no…" Mrs. Cooper began shaking her head, too worried to take on the looks shooting between Jamie and Bea.

Why couldn't he just stay out of this?

"I absolutely *insist* that Mrs. Cooper flies with her son to the hospital," Bea finally interjected as she and Jamie tossed the subject back and forth over Ryan's supine form. No need for the eight-year-old to have a battle over his transport reach epic proportions when all he needed was to hear his mum's voice and the uplifting whir of a helicopter on approach.

"Excuse us for a moment," Jamie said, giving Mrs. Cooper's arm a quick squeeze before rising and tipping his head toward a clearing a few meters away from the triage site. He stopped there and turned to face Bea, his expression deadly serious. "You need to go to the hospital."

"What makes you think that?" She knew she was buying time, but telling Jamie she was pregnant because of a ridiculous cover-up of her ex-fiancé's infertility now...? It would be madness.

Suddenly the shame of it all—the full impact of just how far she had gone to keep the family name golden—hit her like a ton of bricks. Had she really thought she could keep her pregnancy secret? And why should she?

Having this baby was the one good thing that

had come out of that mess and yet here she was again—hiding the truth despite her vow to do otherwise.

Bea blinked, certain she could hear Jamie replying to her question, but all his words were beginning to blur. A swell of nausea began to swirl and rise from her belly as a sharp pain gripped and seized her. She reached out. Her thoughts were muddled. No matter how many times she blinked, her vision was blurring. And as the swell of sensations reached critical mass, darkness fell.

CHAPTER NINE

BEA HEARD THE beeping first.

A heart-rate monitor. She shifted. The sensation of wires sliding along her bare skin brought her to a higher level of alertness. They were taped on. She could feel it now. High up on the exposed skin near her clavicle. On her belly… She wiggled her left hand. There was a clip on her finger.

The heart rate was her own.

Panic seized her and she squeezed her eyes tight shut against the dark thoughts.

Please let my baby be alive!

Not yet ready to open her eyes and face what might be a dark reality, she listened acutely, forcing herself to mark the cadence of the small pips indicating her heart rate.

After a swift rush of high beeps the sounds leveled to a steady rhythm. Faster than normal, but not surprising under the circumstances. She was pregnant. Her heart rate was *meant* to be elevated. Her heart was pumping more blood—an ever-increasing amount as the baby grew—through her womb, her body, her heart.

Beep. Beep. Beep.

Like the beats of a metronome, the heart monitor was telling her she was stable. But all her thoughts were for her child.

Another layer of awareness prickled to attention when she heard light footsteps and the sound of a door opening. Then the sound of Jamie's voice. His wonderful, caramel-rich voice. Assuring a nurse in English that Beatrice must have just had low blood sugar or not enough sleep. He was sure that there wasn't anything to be worried about. Not yet anyway. Best to leave her to rest for a while. In private.

She heard the nurse leave but not Jamie.

For a few blissful moments her thoughts took on a dreamlike quality. She was together with him. They were going to have a child together. Be a family.

Everything in her relaxed, then just as quickly tensed as the click of the door reminded her that they were in the Torpisi Clinic. She was pregnant by a stranger. Her secret was now public.

She swallowed. This was the moment she'd been dreading most. The judgment, the disappointment and ultimately the indifference she was sure she would see in Jamie's eyes.

Her pulse quickened as she heard him approach, tug a wheeled stool across to her bedside. She felt his touch before her eyes fluttered open to see his handsome face.

His hand was lifting to tease away the tendrils of hair no doubt gone completely haywire over her forehead when he noticed she was awake. He pulled his hand away and pushed back from the side of the bed—as if he'd been caught trying to steal a kiss and she were Sleeping Beauty.

If only things were so simple.

Her fingers twitched. Aching to reach out to him. To hold his hand. Feel the warmth of his touch. The desire was urgent. Insatiable. Her hands began to move toward her stomach when fear gripped her. She wasn't ready to go there yet.

"How are you feeling?" Jamie asked from the other side of the room, where he was briskly washing his hands as if scrubbing them with antiseptic would erase everything he'd been thinking or feeling.

She'd heard that tone so many times before. The caring doctor. The doctor who was there to help, but was keeping his emotions in check because he had to.

He shook the water off his hands and turned to her as he toweled them dry.

She parted her lips to speak, surprised at how dry they were. "Thirsty..." she managed, before closing her lids against the deep green of Jamie's eyes.

"Here." He elevated her bed with the electronic toggle. "I've got some water for you."

He handed her the glass, holding the base of it as she took a sip and then braved a glance at him.

Jamie knew. He knew she was pregnant. Why else would he have had her put in a private room? Hooked up monitors to her belly? And yet he still had room in his heart to be kind. Gentle. Caring for her in a moment that was making it more than clear that she'd chosen another over him.

She ached to blurt out the real story. Tell him

it wasn't what he thought. Tell him she'd loved him all along. But to explain the whole ill-conceived story would only diminish what he must already be thinking of her. *Very little.*

She'd seen it in his eyes as the weeks had passed. That famed cool British reserve coming to his rescue time and time again. Just when she'd thought they'd be able to try out a fledgling friendship… *Slam!* Down had gone the shutters, crushing her hope that…that what? She could turn back time and have him back again?

Even the tiny part of her that was still a dreamer didn't stretch *that* far.

"Does your…?" Jamie stopped, swallowed, then began again. "Does he know?"

Bea nodded her head—yes. It was the single blessing she had in this scenario. That man would never be able to lay claim to her child.

But would any other man?

Would Jamie?

"How long have you known?"

She sucked in a deep breath. That was a much harder question to answer. Obviously the treatment had given her more than a ballpark date, but something in her had lit up within days—too early for a test but she had just *known*.

"A couple of months. More…" She was past telling white lies now. All she wanted to know was that her baby was going to be all right.

Just tell him.

Tell him everything.

"I'm guessing you fainted because of lack of food. A bit of dehydration. Sometimes a low iron count can contribute. Have you been taking supplements?"

She nodded. She had. Of course she had. Everything had been done by the book except reducing stress and making sure she always had a snack in hand. But it wasn't as if anyone had anticipated the bus crash. She'd just have to be more careful in the future.

Jamie crossed the room again and tugged open a drawer. He pulled out a little bag of almonds and held them up. "You should keep some snacks on you. At all times. Nuts, cheese, apples… There are all sorts of healthy tidbits you can keep without much bother. It's a bit early, but have you been tested for gestational diabetes?"

Shamefully, she hadn't. Whenever she thought

about the baby she thought about the absurd mess she was in, and went right back to not thinking about it.

"I must've been out a long time," she said finally. "To get back here and not even notice."

"You were." Jamie nodded, his brows cinching together as if he were trying to piece together the bits of puzzle he'd only just been handed. "We got you into an ambulance straightaway. Sometimes when low blood pressure and a handful of other factors collide, fainting is the body's way of rebooting itself. Though it's not like *you* need explanations about what's happening…"

"I'm human as well as a doctor," she said softly. "It's always good to have reminders. An outside eye."

To have you.

Jamie let the words hang there between them without responding.

Bea pressed her back teeth together. It was time to face facts. She was still wearing the khaki pedal pushers she'd had on earlier. There was no telltale wetness between her legs that might indicate that things had gone horribly wrong.

"I didn't take the place of any of the children?"

"No." Jamie sat down on the stool he'd pulled up to Bea's bedside, his eyes on the monitors as he answered. "Most of the children were treated on-site. Those who needed extra care, like Ryan, were flown to Milan. It's easier to get blood supplies there, specialized surgeons, that sort of thing…"

Beatrice couldn't help it. Now that she knew she hadn't elbowed some poor child out of critical transport to a hospital, she blurted out the question she hadn't yet dared to ask. "Is the baby all right?"

"A full exam hasn't been done yet, but if it's miscarriage you're worried about, you can rest easy. I've listened for a heartbeat. Your baby is alive and well."

He sat down on the stool he'd pulled up to her bedside so that they were at eye level. He ran his finger along the rim of her water glass.

Beatrice watched as that finger, long and assured, wound its way along the glass's edge, skidding up and over the area where her lips had touched it. Whether it was a conscious act or not, it stung.

And yet…he had kissed her. Although it was so long ago now it almost felt like a dream.

"Right!" He clapped his hands together. A bit loudly for the small exam room, but it wasn't as if they were having the most casual of exchanges. "How about we take a look together, then?"

Of all the moments Jamie had imagined having with Beatrice, it had never been this.

Giving her an ultrasound scan for a baby that wasn't his.

"Let's get some more water in you. If you can get this whole glass down, we'll be able to see it—your baby—better."

She nodded and started drinking.

He turned to get the screen in place, gather the equipment, willing the years of medical training he'd gone through to kick into action. Enable him to take an emotional step back as he once again turned toward the woman he'd thought he would one day call his wife and apply gel to her belly.

Now that she had unbuttoned her top and shifted her trousers down below her womb, he could see the gentle bump beginning to form. Fighting the urge to reach out and touch it, to lay his fingers wide along the expanse of the soft bulge, Jamie forced himself to rerun the past few weeks like a film on fast-forward.

All the bits of discordant information were coming together now.

Beatrice looking beautifully aglow one moment…gray or near green the next.

The light shadows below her eyes he knew he'd seen more than once… He'd written them off as postwedding stress, but now that he knew she was pregnant…

Everything was out of whack.

"I'm just going to put some gel on."

"It's going to feel cold."

They spoke simultaneously, then laughed. One of those awkward laughs when the jolt of connection reminded a soul just how distanced they'd become from the person they loved. Jamie looked away before he could double-check, but he was fairly certain Beatrice was fighting back tears.

Everything in him longed to pull her into his arms. Comfort her. Hold her. Touch her. Kiss her as he had on that very first day. But how could he now that she was pregnant with *that man's* baby?

Ba-bum. Ba-bum. Ba-bum.

"You hear that?" He kept his eyes solidly on the screen, but despite the strongest will in the universe he felt emotion well up inside him. Beatrice was going to have a child. A beautiful…

"I'm just taking some measurements, here."

"Twelve weeks," she volunteered through the fingers she was pressing to her lips. "It's been about twelve weeks."

The date put the baby's conception date somewhere right around the wedding date. Too close for it to have been a shotgun wedding.

He swallowed away the grim thought. Beatrice might have left him for another man, but he knew in his heart that she never would have cheated on him. On anyone. This child would be Marco's.

"The measurements look good. The baby's about seventy millimeters. A good length."

"Tall?"

"Not overly—but you're tall. The baby's bound to inherit some of your traits."

Her ex-fiancé was tall, as well. Not that he'd spent any time reading the tabloids. Not much anyway.

"Oh, Jamie. Look!" Beatrice's gaze was all unicorns and rainbows as she gazed upon the screen. "She's perfect."

"Or he," Jamie added. It was still a bit early to tell. Maybe two more months. The tail end of Beatrice's contract.

Beatrice was taking no notice of him, waving to the baby. "Hi, there, little girl," she kept repeating. Then to Jamie, more solidly, "She's a little girl. I can tell."

She lifted her hands and moved to caress her belly, only to remember the gel. She pulled them back, accidentally knocking Jamie's arm away from her stomach, and the image dropped from the screen.

"Oh, no! Bring it back! Sorry—please. *Per favore.* Just one more look."

When he turned to look at Beatrice both her hands were covering her mouth, and the tears were trickling freely down and along her cheeks as she took in the fully formed image of her child. All the tiny infant's organs were up and running at this point. Muscles, limbs and bones were in place. Beatrice was showing all the telltale signs of a parent who didn't care one way or the other if a child was a boy or a girl. She was just a mother, thrilled to discover her baby was healthy.

"Do you have plans to tell the father how the baby is doing?"

He didn't know who was more shocked by the question. Himself or Beatrice.

"I—" Bea looked to the black-and-white image on the screen again, then back to Jamie. "He doesn't want anything to do with the child."

"He—he *what*?"

"He didn't—*ugh*!" She scrubbed her hands through her hair. "When I called off the wedding he told me I could do what I liked with the baby."

Saying it out loud made her shiver at the coldness of his words. It was a *life*!

"But—" Jamie shook his head, visibly trying to put the facts in order. "What a coward." Disdain took over where disbelief had creased his features.

"We did it so it would appear to be a honeymoon baby."

The look of pure disbelief was back. Jamie shot it at her and it made her raise her hands to protest, then drop them as if anvils had suddenly fallen into them. "Calling the wedding off wasn't a scenario I had envisioned having to prepare for."

Jamie shook his head, obviously at a total loss for words. She didn't blame him. If she was hearing the same thing from a friend… Well, if it was a friend in similar shoes, from a similar background… She'd heard worse. *Much* worse.

"I know this isn't how things are normally done—"

"Certainly not where *I'm* from," Jamie intoned.

A surge of indignation shot through her. "That's not fair. I've never judged where you've come from. Not in that way."

"You must've judged it to an extent. Decided it—decided *I*—wasn't good enough for you."

All the words drained from Bea's arsenal. "Is that what you think?"

"I think a lot of things, Beatrice, and not one of them involves you getting yourself knocked up by someone who doesn't have the backbone to step up and give a name to his child."

Bea was still reeling from his turn of phrase. "Knocked up?"

It sounded so coarse. Crude, even, the way he'd put it. She might have stooped low to a lot of things, but she had done everything for a reason.

"How dare you? I did this—all of this—for my *family*. Obligation. Duty…" One of her hands pounded into her open one as she continued. "That's how one 'steps up' in a family like *mine*."

For a mother like hers, you upheld tradition. Even when it came at a price.

Jamie took a final glimpse at the image on the screen, then turned to her, his expression an active tempest. The calm of his voice was so still and steady it almost frightened her.

"Beatrice, I don't think I should be involved in this any longer. Perhaps you can find a local obstetrician…?"

"No." She reached out to Jamie as he dropped the scanning wand on the tray next to the monitor and turned away from her. "If the press find out about this they'll have a field day."

"I'm afraid that's really not my concern."

The words landed in her chest like daggers.

"But you—" She stopped herself when she saw his shoulders stiffen and he took another step away from her.

She had no right to ask him for his help.

"This isn't my battle to fight," he said finally, after he'd cleaned his hands and thrown away the paper towels.

He was right. Of course he was right. But something deep inside her wanted to fight this out until there wasn't the tiniest shred of possibility.

Now that he knew everything…

But he didn't know everything. That was the point.

And wasn't his strong reaction because he was feeling the same things she was? Being together. Working together. Having a scan of her baby—

Screech!

Okay. Deep breath. She knew she must be coming across as an absolute screwball now, but the Jamie she knew and loved—

She still loved him. And when you loved someone…did you let them go free or fight?

You fought until there was no choice but to let him go.

"Why did you kiss me?" Bea pushed herself up and looked him straight in the eye. She had to know. Had he felt anything close to the full-on fireworks display she had when their lips had touched for the first time in two years…? Had he felt the magic when physical sensation had melded with powerful emotions and those two forces had joined together?

It had been pure seraphic bliss.

Jamie didn't seem to be taking the same rose-tinted journey down memory lane that she was. Thunder and lightning crashed across his features, rendering his face implacable.

"Everything was different then! I wouldn't have kissed you if I'd known."

"What? So it was all right to kiss me when you thought I was just a runaway bride?"

"You're going to be a *mother*." He turned away to yank some more paper towels from the dispenser.

"It's not what you think."

"Really?" Jamie wheeled on her, eyes flaring

with indignation. "Because I don't believe you have the remotest idea what I'm thinking."

"I have a rough idea," she whispered, no longer able to hold his gaze.

Everything in her longed to run away from this moment. Find another village, another country, another continent to hide away in. But hiding could only last so long. She had a truth to face up to, and until she did she didn't deserve to be a mother, let alone have an ounce of Jamie's respect.

If the last few weeks had taught her anything, it was that hiding the truth from Jamie—no matter how hard she tried—was an impossibility. He was the beacon that drew it from her. Demanded it of her. He was her true north and she owed him an honest answer.

She stretched her arms out toward him, knowing he wouldn't fall into them as she ached for him to do, but at least the gesture would speak a thousand words she couldn't voice.

Jamie shook his head, refusing to move any closer.

"How can you have even the slightest idea of what I am thinking, Beatrice? Your life…

You've made decisions that took away any right to know what I'm thinking."

"Those decisions had nothing to do with how I felt about you, though."

"How could they not?" He spread his arms out wide and looked around the room, as if there were a crowd assembled in a courtroom. A jury keen to pass judgment one way or the other. "You *left* me, Beatrice. Left me to marry another man. Now, I'm sorry it didn't pan out the way you envisioned it, but you're pregnant by another man and, like it or not, he's going to be part of your future."

"But I'm *not*."

Jamie gave his head a sharp shake, his hands latching onto his hips. "What do you mean you're not? We saw the baby. Alive and kicking." He pointed to the scan where the black-and-white image remained. "Whose is it if not his?"

"I don't know."

Bea's chest nearly exploded with relief. She'd said it. Said it and it nothing had happened. Well, nothing yet anyway, because Jamie's jaw was twitching and she knew what *that* meant. He had something to say, but he was going to wait until he was ready so that whatever it was would come out with surgical precision.

Before he leapt to any other conclusions she began explaining. She told him everything. About her ex-fiancé's infertility. The high expectations for a honeymoon baby. The demand for a male heir to the Rodolfo name. Their agreement for her to have the IVF treatment. The moment she'd walked away after discovering his infidelity.

Despite the gravity of the situation, she burst out laughing. "Isn't it hilarious that she's going to be a girl?"

"We're not going to know that for another eight weeks."

"We?"

The word hung between them like an offer of something more.

Everything in him fought to return Beatrice's smile.

We.

Two little letters.

Far too much history.

Though she didn't move, he heard the word again.

It ran over and over in his mind, as if he was trying to extract every ounce of meaning he could from the moment.

Her voice was full of hope. *Hell!* He could see it in her beautiful brown eyes. Trace it through the flush pinking up her cheeks, its heat adding even more red to her full lips.

But what was she asking of him? To forget the past? Forget that she had chosen her family and another man over him? The thought riled him.

Family, eh?

That wasn't how family worked where *he* came from.

After all his family had done for him—the sacrifices they had made—he would have a hard time telling them where to go if they didn't approve of the woman he loved. Maybe…

No. This was an entirely different scenario now. Perhaps Beatrice was good old-fashioned scared. He was a familiar entity, and she didn't want to go through this alone. But another man's child? A stranger's?

The way this whole crazy story was unfurling, Jamie couldn't help but think Beatrice was a stranger to him now. The woman he'd known wouldn't have done any of those things. It was time she owned up to her behavior. Accepted some responsibility.

"I think you should try to find the father," he said finally, after the silence became unbearable.

Beatrice threw him an odd look. "He's anonymous."

"What?" Confusion rained through him like nails. "Did aliens come down to earth, abduct the Beatrice I knew and once truly loved and replace her with *you*?"

She stared at him for a moment. As if processing the accusations. The facts. But he knew it wasn't as if any of this rang true with the woman he'd once known. The time he'd spent with Beatrice had definitely been a fairy tale compared to this nightmare.

Beatrice sat up in the bed, pulling her shirt closer around herself even though the monitors were all still attached. She reached unsuccessfully for a blanket at the foot of the bed, and for one not very nice second Jamie felt like picking it up and throwing it over her. Just hiding her away from sight.

"The treatment was anonymous."

He blinked and forced himself to pull her back into focus. Her eyebrows tugged together, then lifted, her expression changing into something a bit brighter. "I did stipulate that, whoever he was, he must have at least a drop of English heritage."

The words slammed him in the chest and sucked out the oxygen when he heard himself echoing Beatrice. "English?"

"English," Bea repeated, her eyes solidly on his as she gave a wicked little laugh. "That was my little secret at the clinic. No one knows—well, now you know…but no one else knows." She gave her stomach a reassuring pat and pulled her top down close, as if to warm it.

If possible, the atmosphere in the small exam room flexed and then strained against the swirl of information Jamie was trying to make sense of.

A flash of a future that might have been his slammed into his solar plexus. *He* should be the one fathering that little boy or girl growing in Beatrice's womb. *He* should be the one to soothe it, rock it to sleep while his wife caught up on her sleep. He should be the one to tickle its nose, read stories in the middle of the night even though he or she wouldn't be ready yet to hear about Treasure Island or Cinderella. Holding the tiny infant in his arms.

The tug of longing he felt in his chest near enough suffocated him. The harsh reality was that it *wasn't* his child. And it wasn't his future to dream about.

"Your fi—how did he become infertile?"

Bea's shoulders lifted and collapsed in a deep sigh. "I'd love to make a joke about Italian men and tight underwear, but it's a bit more complicated than that."

"He didn't—he wasn't unsafe with you, was he? Did he hurt you at all?"

Jamie fought the urge to go to her, pull her into his arms, instead channeling all his energy into tightening his fingers along the counter's edge—as if pressing the blood out of himself would make her revelations hurt less.

Why hadn't he done more to keep her by his side?

You just let her go.

"No." Beatrice shook her head, her upper lip curling a bit, as if she were reliving an unpleasant memory. "We never consummated our relationship. For a number of reasons."

Her features changed, as if even saying the words was akin to tasting the most sour of fruits.

As quickly as she'd sunk into a sigh she sat up tall, charged with an invisible shot of energy. "I need to get out of here."

She tugged off the monitor tabs and turned her back to Jamie. Shirt buttoned and tucked into her trousers, after a quick swipe and clean of the gel that had so recently helped give them access to that little baby inside her, she turned to him with a renewed sense of purpose flaring in her dark eyes.

"Jamie, listen. My cousin has offered me the use of his chalet in the next valley over. It's blissful. I went there once in the winter season. I have a couple of days scheduled off. Is there any chance I could convince you to come with me? Let me explain everything. Give you a chance to ask all the questions you must have."

A knock sounded on the door. The nurse called in and said that she had an update about a couple of the children who had been flown to Milan and one who was here at the clinic.

Jamie wanted more than anything to ignore it. To go to this "blissful" chalet and start asking the pileup of questions jamming in his throat. See if there was even the tiniest sliver of hope that they could start something new.

But he wasn't there yet. Couldn't pair the woman he'd loved with the one in front of him—drowning him in a flood of off-key information.

"Sorry." He pulled a fresh white coat off of the back of the door. "Duty calls."

An hour, later Bea felt ready. Refreshed after a restorative walk along the lakeshore and a power nap that seemed to have supercharged her.

She was ready to fight for her baby. *And* for her man.

When Jamie stepped out of the back door of the clinic he looked exhausted. More tired than she'd ever seen him. And she knew it had nothing to do with work. The second their gazes connected, she knew her battle to win him over was already lost.

"Shouldn't you be at home? Resting?"

The words in another context, another tone would have been soothing. Caring even. But at the sound of the brittle tone they'd been delivered in all the impassioned reasons to try again Bea had planned to stack at his feet like Christmas presents were swept away.

"I thought I'd come in and do a couple of hours. Relieve anyone who was at the crash site."

"I think it's best if you don't." Jamie squared his stance to hers. "I know your contract runs until the end of the summer—early September, wasn't it?"

She nodded, her tongue weighted to the bottom of her mouth with disbelief. *He was going to fire her.*

Not wanting to hear what was coming next, she shook her fingers in a wide just-stop gesture that anyone with half a brain could have read.

And yet he continued, as if purging a poison from his own body.

"I think it's best if you don't come in anymore. I'm sure we'll be able to get through the next few days with relief staff. Until we can get someone permanent in."

He spoke as if in a trance. The words coming

out in the dull, staccato tones of an automaton. As if his hollowed-out heart would never know the joy of love again.

Part of her wanted to rush to him. Take her hand and press it to his chest, feel for the beat of his heart. She knew it was there. Knew blood pumped through his veins the same as hers. And yet…

This Jamie frightened her.

This Jamie was saying goodbye.

"If you've left anything, I'll get someone to bring it by. I presume you'll stay in town overnight?"

Her shoulders slumped with defeat as she watched his cool gaze drop to her lips, then to the dip of her clavicle. The swoop of bone and flesh he'd used to trace with the pad of his thumb before dipping his head to press hot kisses into the hollow at the base of her throat.

Heat clashed with icy cold as the sensation of his gaze and the memory of his touch collided.

She shut her eyes against the memory, willing herself to focus on the child she was carrying. The love she and Jamie had once shared.

And when she opened her eyes again…willing to bare her soul to him for one last shot at being together…he was gone.

CHAPTER TEN

BEA PULLED THE covers around her shoulders, not quite ready to admit that it was morning even though the sun was already peeking through the shutters she could never bring herself to close.

Bah! Who needed another sunny day when it was raining inside her head?

Pragmatism told her that her behavior was bordering on depression.

Her heart said otherwise.

She'd laid it on the line. As good as reached into her own chest and handed Jamie her heart with a ribbon and bow on it and a little tag attached. *Take me.*

She pulled the sheet up and over her head and gave a small groan. She'd already cried as many tears as her body would allow. Cried until she'd fallen asleep. And even then it had been restless, fraught with terrifying dreams. Darkness. Unseen dangers. Cliff edges. Racing vehicles. Natural disasters. Anything and everything she'd ever been frightened of gathered together in a dream to lure her into the most harrowing of chases for survival.

Well…

She cracked an eye open and let the morning sounds of the town register.

She'd survived.

Just.

There was a part of her that still wanted to curse Jamie. Scream at him for not standing by her at this time of crazy, urgent need. The other half of her knew she had no right. All of this was a nightmare of her own making.

All of it save her inability to stop loving him.

It was time to let go. She knew it now.

No matter how cruel his looks, how callous his words, she knew she would love Jamie until the end of time. It was as if the first time she'd met him, he'd lit a single candle in the center of her heart. A pure flame that had refused—no matter what she had thrown at it—to be extinguished.

True love could never die.

But perhaps it could change form.

The harsh, unforgiving speeches she would

normally be giving herself were impossible to drum up.

Had she…? Was this her first step in forgiving herself?

Her hands slipped to her belly. The only way she could go on was to forgive herself for all she had done. Everything—no matter how insane it had seemed—had been done with love in her heart.

Had it landed her in the deep end?

Most definitely.

Would she make it to the other side?

A smile tweaked at the edges of her lips.

Of course she would.

No matter how down she felt, it was time to find the reserves of strength lying somewhere deep within her and protect and care for the baby she was carrying on her own.

The phone rang and she let out a groan. Anyone who knew her would hear that her throat had been rasped raw with sobbing the night away. Maybe she should call in sick.

A fresh bloom of tears clouded her eyes.

There was no work.

She'd been unceremoniously fired.

Sighing, she batted her hand about on the bedside table until she hit the phone and pulled it under the covers.

"Pronto?"

"Don't go out this morning."

Bea sat straight up in bed, pulling the covers around her as if they would shield her from whatever news he was about to spill.

"Jamie?" She knew it was him, but the message he was conveying wasn't computing at all.

"The press. They're all around your *baita*. The clinic, too. They got a photo."

"Photo?" She shook her head, the information still not entirely registering.

"Of you… Me. Your hand on your belly."

She shook her head again, willing her brain to play along. Sort everything into the right place.

"When?"

One-word responses seemed to be all she was capable of this morning.

"Yesterday at the accident scene. There was press everywhere."

Her fingers flew to her mouth. Of *course* there had been. She'd been so engrossed in work she hadn't even thought to consider…

The accident scene came back to her in vivid snapshots.

Emergency tape cordoning off the onlookers… Had there been photographers among the crowd? Mobile phones?

Definitely.

The flash of cameras as they lost the light?

Paparazzi at a crash site?

Or a keen-eyed tourist trying to make some extra money.

Had anyone called out her name?

She shook her head again. It was so hard to remember.

Helicopters flying in and out.

One helicopter hovering… Something a medical chopper would never do… *Press.*

A man on a motorcycle, trying to talk his way past the *polizia di stato* overseeing the slow flow of traffic trickling down the mountainside past the crash site. He'd had a camera, long lensed, resting on his thigh…and then she'd stumbled.

She squeezed her eyes tight against the memory.

"Beatrice?" Jamie's caramel-rich voice was edged with worry. "Are you still there?"

"*Si*—yes." A logjam of words caught in her throat, and in the end all she achieved was a cry for help. "I—I'm not sure what to do."

"I know what you're *not* going to do…" And in a steady, assured voice, Jamie began detailing how to get out of this outrageous predicament.

She let his voice do what it always did. Pour down her insides like warm caramel, pooling at the base of her spine where it turned molten. Fiery. A lava-hot core of resolve.

Bea swung her legs out of bed, pressing her toes against the cool wooden planks of her apartment, taking strength from his assured tone that she would be fine.

"Close your shutters. Take a nice shower. Put on a loose-fitting dress. Find a hat. If you don't have one, I'll bring one."

"You'll bring one? What are you talking about?"

"I'm coming over. Don't open your door to anyone but me."

"Jamie, what are you talking about? I thought—"

I thought you wanted me out of your life.

"Never mind what I thought. I can't have my

patients' welfares compromised because of the press outside."

Ah.

The patients. Of course.

"I'm going to drive up to the back door. Your landlord will let me in. Don't even be tempted to leave your apartment until you're certain it's me."

"It's really not your concern."

"It is now," he bit back, his voice as grim as she'd ever heard it. "You made it my concern the second you stepped into my clinic."

He was lashing out. She knew that. He'd never asked for everything she'd brought in her wake.

Her eyes worked their way over to the suitcases she'd already packed, the clothes she'd set out to make an early departure, before the full impact of Jamie's demand that she leave had kept her cemented to her bed.

She would leave on her own. No matter how hard it would be not to fight for the man she loved with all her heart, the life she'd thought they could share together, she would leave so *he* could survive.

"I'll get a taxi." She flicked an app open on

her *telefono*. "There's a train leaving in a half an hour. I'll be on it. Just—" She swallowed back the tears stinging her raw throat. "It's really okay."

"It really *isn't*, Beatrice."

Why was he making this more difficult than he had to? For both of them?

"I've already spoken to the local police about an escort. Do you know the fastest way to your cousin's chalet? The one you mentioned yesterday? I can get some security in place before we arrive if you let me know what the address is."

"Wait! *We?*"

Leaving on her own was going to be harrowing enough. She'd just made the tiniest of baby steps toward making peace with herself and already it was torn to shreds. *Deep breath in...*

"Jamie. Surely I can get past a couple of paparazzi on my own? I know I'm no pro, but I have managed a few in my time."

"Beatrice, there are *dozens* of them."

Jamie's words crystalized in her brain as he spoke…then froze icy cold as he continued.

"Even more here at the clinic. You're trapped."

The phone clattered to the floor as her hands

instinctively wove around her belly, protecting the tiny life inside. The fist-sized baby she'd vowed to take care of no matter what.

Something fierce and powerful rose within her. A mother's elemental chemistry at work, protecting what she and she alone could give life to. This was *her* battle. And hers alone.

She scooped the phone from the floor, took swift strides to the windows and pulled the shutters closed against the invasive glare of the tabloid press. There was an underground garage she could leave through. Calls she could make.

Part of her felt like striding out in front of them all, holding a press conference, pouring her heart out so the world would know once and for all that being a princess was far from living "less than a whisper away from heaven," as one of the tabloids had put it right before her disastrous wedding.

"I got myself into this mess. Thank you for your help."

She parted her lips again to wish him well in life, but stopped herself because the only words she knew would come tumbling out if she continued would be the three most beautiful and yet cuttingly painful words of all…

I love you.

She held the phone away from her ear and with great remorse pressed the little red symbol that would end the call. Then swiftly, through the blur of tears now flowing freely down her cheeks, she deleted the number.

It felt like cutting off a limb. But at long last she felt pride at her decision. A long-awaited fragment of self-respect that she knew would only continue to grow.

Jamie stared at the phone with an equal mix of terror and fury churning through his veins.

She'd hung up on him.

He was trying to *help*!

Surely she could see he was trying to help.

He stuffed the phone into his pocket, his gaze snagging on the tabloid newspaper in front of him. The picture took up nearly three quarters of the page. Beatrice was front and center. She was wearing the regulation emergency-care jump-suit, so it wasn't obvious she was pregnant. Even now he knew it was still difficult to tell. There was a soft arc where he'd scanned her belly yesterday, but nothing so pronounced it was obvious. And yet…

He shook his head, willing himself not to relive the moment where he'd first laid eyes on the child growing inside Beatrice's womb. *Useless.* No matter what he did—eyes open, closed, half-mast—none of it worked. He could still see that baby—still feel the thread of empathy… *No.* It wasn't empathy. He'd seen hundreds of babies inside hundreds of wombs in the course of his medical career, and held even more in his arms as a pediatrician.

But he'd never felt for any of them what he'd felt for this one.

Love.

Electricity crackled through him as the thought took shape and grew.

Of *course* he loved the child.

Because he loved Beatrice.

It was why he hadn't been able to sleep. Why everything, despite being in the full bloom of summer, had seemed gray, dull and lifeless since he'd all but kicked her out of the clinic. Of his life.

It explained his ridiculous knight in shining armor attempt. By telephone.

The memory curdled when he tried to give it a softer edge.

It had been little less than cowardly.

He had given himself a way out by ringing Beatrice from the safety of his office, instead of elbowing his way past all those ridiculous camera-wielding journalists. Beatrice was right to have hung up on him. They were photographers—not armed snipers lying in wait to kill anyone.

Though they *were* stealing her right to live her life the way she chose. Just as he'd done by rejecting the baby she was going to bring into the world.

She wasn't mad. Or foolish. She was brave. Loving. Selfless, even, to bring a child created in such calculated circumstances into the world and love it as if she *hadn't* lost everything in the process.

A fire started in his gut. Beatrice shouldn't have to do this. Hide away from the press. Sneak out of her shuttered apartment under the cover of darkness or hidden behind another disguise. Be fired for being—what?—the love of his life?

So she was pregnant because of an attempt to do the right thing by a family so interwoven in the traditions of the past that she'd agreed out of loyalty?

He knew loyalty.

He showed it to his patients. He gave it willingly to his own family. Would lay down his life for them.

He glanced at the newspaper again.

> Mystery Knight in Shining Armor for Venice's Runaway Principessa!

Hardly pithy, but no one needed to read the wordy headline to understand the one thing that photo showed.

He was in love with Beatrice.

It was there for all the world to see.

She was reaching out as the darkness of her faint began to consume her, and the expression on Jamie's face as he stretched out his arms to catch her was one of the harrowing anxiety of a man who would lose a part of himself if he lost her.

* * *

There was no chance Bea was going to risk another set of heartbroken-princess headlines.

Jilted Again!

Always the Fiancée…Never the Bride!

Destined to be Alone…Forever.

Well, screw that!

If she was going to leave, she was going to leave with her head held high.

One long shower, a session in front of the mirror and a bit of prevarication over the blue dress that flattered her olive skin or the green that definitely showed her small baby bump later…and she was ready to go.

Her heart rate accelerated as the elevator doors opened to the wide foyer on the ground floor of her apartment block…the last open space before she opened the doors to the world…

"Jamie?"

She looked over her shoulder, as if half expecting the press to jump out of some invisible closet and scream "Surprise!" All the while snapping away, taking photos of her looking shocked.

But there was no one. No one except for Jamie, standing there as handsome as ever, blond hair curling over the edges of his shirt collar, green eyes holding her in their steady gaze.

Her gut instinct was to run to him, throw herself into his arms and weep with relief that she wouldn't have to go through any sort of charade with the press. The other instinct? The other instinct was hopping mad that he was there at all.

Wasn't *he* the one who had pointed the way to the exit yesterday?

Wasn't *he* the one who had refused to consider trying again?

Wasn't *he* the one to whom she had lost her heart all those years ago and against whom no one else would compare? *Ever.*

She put one foot in front of the other and made her way across the foyer, through the doors and out onto the street, Jamie keeping pace with her the entire time. He swept out in front of her, down the steps and toward his car.

"Madame..." He opened the passenger door of his dark blue 4x4—a typical rugged Alpine doc vehicle. "Your carriage awaits."

Bea stayed rooted to the spot. *No way.* She

wasn't going to let her heart go on this crazy merry-go-round ride again. She'd been through enough emotional joyrides and not a single one of them had been fun.

"What did you do?" she heard herself ask in a voice that didn't sound natural.

Jamie had the grace to look the tiniest bit bashful before he admitted, "I told them you'd left the clinic and were headed to Milan. Something about going to a hospital ward..."

The edges of her lips twitched. But he didn't deserve to win her smile. Not yet anyway.

"What type of ward?" she asked, her fingers still retaining their firm grip on the handles of her wheeled luggage.

"A maternity ward," he answered, the twinkle in his green eyes flashing bright.

The tiniest glimmer of hope formed in her chest.

"Oh, really? And what is it exactly I'm meant to be doing there?"

"I don't think you'll be doing *anything* there," he answered, his voice growing thick with emotion. He tipped his head toward the car. "What do you say we get you out of here? Before they figure out someone might've given them duff information."

Her hand swept to her belly. She couldn't do this again. Not if he was just offering her a ride to so-called freedom. It would just be a few days in a holding pattern until she came up with a new plan. A new place to hide away.

That wasn't how she was going to face life anymore. She was a handful of months away from being a single mother. It was time to stand on her own two feet. Even so…he *was* looking terribly earnest. It would be rude not to ask what his plan was.

Wouldn't it?

She gave her hair an unnecessary shake and showed him her haughtiest look.

"What exactly are you proposing, Jamie?"

"I'm proposing we get out of here," he said, taking a determined step toward her. "I'm proposing you consider forgiving me for acting like a boor."

Bea shivered despite the warm summer breeze as he took yet another step. Only a handful of stairs stood between them. She had a chance. A chance to turn around…flee. Escape with a bit of her heart intact.

Her fingers pressed against the warm curve of her belly.

"I'm also proposing," he continued, taking the steps in a few swift, long-legged strides and pulling her hands into his, "that we get out of here before any straggling paparazzi come by. C'mon!"

He tipped his head toward the car and reached either side of her to pick up her bags. She caught a warm hit of evergreen and…honey? Candle wax? She'd never been able to put a finger on it, but the scent had always been Jamie.

She would accept the ride and then she would say goodbye.

Loving a stranger's baby was a big ask. Just knowing he'd forgiven her, knowing she could leave with true peace between them, stilled her restless heart.

He dropped her a wink. "C'mon. I know a girl who has a cousin who has a chalet somewhere out there in the wilderness. Let's get out of here."

Jamie knew the only way to stop himself from popping the question on the torturously long thirty-minute car ride was to fill the car with opera. Beatrice loved listening to the beautiful arias of Puccini, so he scanned his phone's music library until he found the file he'd been unable to delete when she'd left.

Even catching a glimpse of it had been like swallowing bile up until today. But today? Seeing it there on his phone was like receiving a hit of much-needed sunshine on a rainy day.

As if he'd called up to the heavens and ordered it the clouds shifted away one by one until, when at long last they reached the hidden-away chalet, the sky was a beautiful clear blue and the sun shone brightly down on the broad spread of mountain meadows surrounding the estate.

Beatrice gave him the code for the gate, and when they drew up to the house she turned to him, her face taut with nerves. "You'd probably be best just leaving me here. I'll be all right."

"I am not doing any such thing, Beatrice di Jesolo."

He was out of the car before she could stop him and around at her side, opening the door and pulling her hands into his as he dropped to one knee.

"I was hoping not to do this next to the footwell of a beat-up 4x4, but if there's one thing I've learned this summer it's that waiting is a bad idea when it comes to you."

Beatrice's brow crinkled. "What do you mean?"

"I was a first-class idiot, Beatrice. Two years ago when you left I should've put up a fight. Proved I was the man for you. Maybe I wasn't. But I've grown a lot since then."

A dark sigh left his chest, leaving the bright hope of possibility in its wake.

"And I hope you will believe me when I say I've grown the most since you've come back into my life."

"What is it you're saying, Jamie?"

"I'm saying I love you. I'm saying I want to marry you. I've *always* wanted to marry you. I'm saying I want to be a father to the child you're carrying and any other babies you and I might create as we live out our lives of wedded bliss."

He pulled her hands into his and dropped kisses on each of them.

"We've missed too much time together, Beatrice. Time I don't want to risk losing again. Please say you'll marry me?"

He looked straight into her eyes, praying that what was beating in her heart was the same fiery, undying passion beating in his own.

"Beatrice di Jesolo, will you do me the honor of becoming my wife?"

For one heart-stopping moment a crease of distress flashed across her features, before dissolving into the most beautiful smile he'd ever seen.

"You're absolutely sure?"

"Positively."

"My family is insane."

"Mine is *too* sane," he countered. "It'll make a nice balance."

"Your mother-in-law will be a very…uniquely challenging woman," she said warningly.

"I've been told I have a way with the ladies." He dropped a wink and rose to his feet so he could look her square in the face. "I'll win her over."

Beatrice's eyebrows lifted. "You have to win the bride over first."

"So it's a yes?"

"This *is* what you want?" she asked. "Mystery baby and all?"

She gently pulled her hands from his and swept them along the small swell beneath her cotton dress.

"Mystery baby and all," he replied, more solidly than he could even have imagined. He meant it. He wanted this baby. To love it. To raise it. To read stories to it while it was still in the womb and for every day after. "You are the love of my life, Beatrice. I can't let you get away again."

Tears popped inito her eyes as she nodded her understanding. "*Si, amore*. It's a yes."

He didn't need to hear another word. Whooping with joy, he swung her around before pulling her into his arms for a kiss that was long overdue.

Sweet, sensual, loving, impassioned… The kiss embodied it all.

When at long last they broke apart, heads tipped together as if any more space between them was an impossibility, he whispered to her again, "I love you, Beatrice."

"I love you, too, Jamie. Forever and a day."

EPILOGUE

BEA PUSHED THE shutters back so that the morning sun could flood into the bedroom, barely able to contain her fizz of expectation. January in Britain had never seemed so beautiful. Frost still covered the fields beyond the house—just as Jamie had described when he'd told her about the single winter he'd spent here on his own, with only the wood burner for company.

Well, a lot had changed since then.

A knock sounded at her bedroom door, and before she could cross to answer it Fran's face appeared in the door frame, wreathed in smiles.

"And how is the happy bride-to-be?"

"Happy!" Bea said, laughing as she spoke, feeling another jolt of enthusiasm crackling through her veins. She beckoned Francesca in and twirled around. "What do you think?"

"Beautiful!" Fran's fingers flew to her lips as emotion stemmed anything else she'd planned to say. "Jamie's going to go wild with desire when he sees you!"

"Hardly!" Bea swatted at the air between them, allowing herself a little twist and twirl to show off the A-line cap-sleeved dress she still couldn't believe she fitted into. "Eight and a half months pregnant, swollen feet and chubby cheeked is *not* how I was expecting to walk down the aisle."

"Oh, don't be silly," Francesca parried, flopping onto the old-fashioned bed with an added bounce or two. "You tried it the other way and that was clearly not singular enough for you. Surely your mother—"

"Uh-uh! No, you don't!" Bea feigned horror as she turned to her hodgepodge of a dressing table, pulled together from a packing box and a precariously balanced mirror she'd found in the attic a couple of hours earlier.

She lowered herself onto the packing crate in front of it, ensuring she swept the short train of champagne-colored fabric to the side as she found purchase on the slats. Her mother would be having an absolute hissy fit if she could see her right now.

"We already tried it her way, and the reason

you're here and not her is because I thought I could rely on you not to go all Principessa royal this, royal that on me. We both know that is *not* a recipe for success."

"I don't know..." Fran pushed herself up from the bed and wandered over to stand behind her friend, their gazes connecting in the mirror. "It worked out pretty well for Luca and me."

"You and Luca have an entire village at your disposal!"

Fran's musical laugh filled the room. "It was a great day, wasn't it?"

"Amazing. Enough glamor to tide my mother over until my brother decides to get married."

"*Pfft!* Hardly!" Fran rolled her eyes. "I suppose Dad *did* go a bit over-the-top with the catering, didn't he?"

"You should see what *my* father brought over. His suitcase was full of food and nothing else!" Bea's hand swept across the arc of her swollen tummy. "*Oof!* I think this baby girl is going to be part focaccia and part wedding cake if the past few weeks are anything to go by! Italian made, that's for sure!"

Fran took up a lock of Bea's hair and started

weaving it into an intricate plait along her hairline. "You're still convinced it's going to be a girl?"

"She," Bea answered solidly. "I'm sure of it."

"I thought you weren't going to find out?"

"We haven't, but… You should know by now—a mother can sense things."

Fran stepped to Bea's side and put her hands on her own growing belly. "It's madness, isn't it? The two of us pregnant at the same time?"

"Jamie would say it's the world proving to us that we can show our mothers how it's *really* done."

"Jamie would say anything to make sure you're here with him in this beautiful home, about to embark on a beautiful life together." Fran grinned, returning to her role as wedding hairdresser. "It's so great the hospital is only a fifteen-minute drive away."

"Mmm…" Bea nodded. "Great for work and great for when my water breaks!"

"I can't believe how much your hair has grown. It's *so* beautiful now." Fran pulled an apologetic face in the mirror and rapidly covered. "I mean the platinum thing was good for a while, but—"

"Well, you're not supposed to dye it when you're pregnant, are you? And it wasn't really *me*," Bea said, pulling a face in the mirror. "A lot of things weren't me over the past couple of years, but now…?"

She looked around the huge old high-ceilinged room, its corners stacked with boxes yet to be unpacked. Only the antique bed and the cradle beside it—lying in wait for its little occupant to make an entrance—were already made up and ready for use.

"Now I'm finally at home."

Jamie glanced at his watch again, his brow crinkling further when Luca gave a rich, throaty laugh.

"Relax!" He clapped an arm around the nervous groom. "I thought the whole point of having your wedding at your house was so you could enjoy yourself!"

"It would be *completely* enjoyable if my bride would ever—" Whatever else he'd been going to say vanished. There, at the doorway to their centuries-old sitting room, was an angel.

Beatrice had never looked so beautiful. Her

dark hair had been magicked into an intricate updo. Miniscule little plaits and curls of mahogany hair outlined her perfect face. Lips full and pinkened with emotion rather than lipstick. He knew she hadn't put on a lick of makeup since she and her mother had agreed to disagree on "the true aesthetic of a princess." The swoop and swell of her stomach made his heart skip a beat.

A husband and a father all in the space of a month.

The celebrant they had chosen for their simple ceremony cleared his throat, and Beatrice's father jumped up from the armchair where he'd been making friends with Francesca and Luca's latest canine companion.

"Beatrice! *Amore...*" He raised a fist to his mouth to stem a sob. "You look beautiful," he added in English as he reached out his arm for her to take.

There was only a handful of steps to take from the doorway to just in front of the French windows, looking out onto the sprawling back garden and the farmers' fields beyond, but with each step Beatrice took Jamie felt his heart pound with greater conviction and pride than he thought he had ever felt before.

When Beatrice's father dropped a kiss onto his daughter's cheek and passed her hand over to Jamie's he whispered something in Italian—clearly meant for his future son-in-law's hearing. Jamie's mind was too scrambled to translate it perfectly, but he got the gist. *Take care of my little girl.*

He gave him a nod. There was nothing that would stop him from loving and protecting the woman by his side ever again.

Time took on an otherworldly quality, and it seemed that just a few moments later Jamie was pulling his beautiful wife in to him with one hand, while the other tipped her chin up so he could seal their wedding vows with a kiss.

When at last they broke apart he swept the tears of joy from her cheeks as the tiniest wedding party in history applauded their brand-new union.

"Are you ready to start your life as Mrs. Coutts?" he asked before they stepped away from the "altar."

"Only if you're ready to go and get the car

keys," she replied, both her hands swooping over the rich arc of champagne fabric swaddling her belly as she sucked in a sharp intake of breath.

"Are you…?" Jamie looked at the other faces in the room, each as wide-eyed as he was. "Do you mean we…?"

Beatrice nodded, the smile on her face near enough reaching from ear to ear. "A husband *and* a father. All on the same day!"

Jamie ran a few steps toward the Victorian-tiled foyer for the keys, then doubled back to his brand-new wife and took her hand in his, forcing himself to take a steadier pace as they walked to the door.

He barked out orders to Fran to get Beatrice's shawl, to Beatrice's bemused father to find the prepacked suitcase and to Luca to grab the wedding cake.

"You planned this, didn't you?" he whispered into his wife's ear. "The best wedding present of all."

She answered with a kiss, and by the time they had broken apart everyone had whirled into action and it were in place to head off to the hospital for an entirely new escapade as husband and wife.

"Mrs. Coutts?" Jamie swept open the door and scooped up his wife. "I know this isn't the doorway you were expecting to go through after we were married, but are you ready for the next stage of our adventure?"

"With you by my side?" she asked, nestling into the crook between his chin and shoulder. "Every day for the rest of my life."

* * * * *

If you enjoyed this story, check out these other great reads from Annie O'Neil

HEALING THE SHEIKH'S HEART
HER HOT HIGHLAND DOC
SANTIAGO'S CONVENIENT FIANCÉE
THE NIGHTSHIFT BEFORE CHRISTMAS

All available now!